Mister Piper and Me

Joe R. Tueller

ISBN 0-7414-3230-7

Cover Artwork: "The Yellow Airplane" by Bryan Hammond.

Published by:

PUBLISHING.COM

*1094 New DeHaven Street, Suite 100
West Conshohocken, PA 19428-2713
Info@buybooksontheweb.com
www.buybooksontheweb.com
Toll-free (877) BUY BOOK
Local Phone (610) 941-9999
Fax (610) 941-9959*

Printed in the United States of America

Printed on Recycled Paper

Published May 2006

Dedications

For Kristine, daughter and former copilot.

Chapter 1

It was late afternoon, on that spring day in 1938, when the small yellow airplane came drifting low over the valley floor. It looked down upon fields that formed a patchwork quilt in greens and browns. All features—trees, fences, farm buildings—stood out in sharp relief, accentuated by their stretching shadows. The storm that had passed the night before had washed everything sparkling clean. Bold colors seemed almost luminescent in intensity.

The long wings tilted one way and then the other in slow cadence—a graceful lifting and falling of a dancer's arms—as the craft frolicked in the quiet air. Grazing cattle took note of its weaving approach. A few ran frightened with tails high, soon to stop and stand, wide-legged and bug-eyed, while the apparition passed overhead.

Approaching the edge of town it began a gradual turn away from the community. Abruptly it swerved from this path and started to circle a figure who had come into view in the pasture below. Lying on the grass, next to a tiny creek, her yellow slacks and blue blouse contrasted distinctly with the surrounding green. She could be seen rising to a sitting position with upturned face following the airplane. After a few circuits she waved and then stood to wave again.

Around and around it went until it seemed that the earth had commenced to spin under a fixed platform in the sky. Then the wings leveled and the craft floated away to the south. Soon it began the slow, weaving waltz that had characterized its arrival—wings alternately dipping and rising, reflecting bright yellow in the evening sun.

* * *

Katie Stuart had been startled by the clatter of the engine. With her face buried in the grass that grew long next to

1

the creek and her senses dulled by emotional turmoil, she had failed to hear the airplane until it was almost overhead. Panic seized her with the illusion that Bart's tractor was bearing down on her position and she sat up quickly.

"Wha . . . ?" In her confusion, a part of her mind asked what he was doing with his tractor in the pasture. She looked around frantically for the source of the noise. Then, brushing away tears, she saw it.

Her sorrow was immediately forgotten when she realized that the airplane was flying around her as if it was being whirled on a string. The wing, like a pointing finger, was directed at the exact place where she sat, so that she saw only the tip. So close was the craft that its individual parts could be easily distinguished: the little wheels, a propeller that showed as a blur in the sunlight, the windows.

The windows held her attention. There were three on the side back of the windshield. Somehow she had never given much thought to the people inside airplanes she had observed flying high over the valley. There seemed little relationship between people and a speck in the sky. But here, a few hundred yards away, she could see clearly the man behind the rearmost window. And he was looking at her!

His head and upper body were silhouetted against the sky and she watched him on his orbital track, wondering what he saw of the girl sitting on the grass. Did he think she was older than her seventeen years, or younger? Did he think she might be pretty? He couldn't know from up there that she was a little too tall and a little too thin and that her legs were a little too long. Only grandpa called her pretty, but that didn't count. He had always called her pretty. Self–consciously she lifted a hand to her short, sun–bleached hair, then higher in a timid wave. A hand moved behind the windows. With that, she waved more vigorously and was answered.

As the circling continued, Katie stood and pivoted to watch the flight. She made great exaggerated arm–waving motions and laughed, not heeding the dizziness that was starting. Staggering, she laughed again remembering the child she had been, spinning and spinning until she fell down.

But suddenly the airplane straightened and flew away.

Disappointed, she watched the wagging wings go off to the south, diminishing in size until only a dot remained. Finally even that was gone.

Who is he? Where did he come from? Where is he going? These thoughts tumbled over and over in her mind.

She stood for a long time searching the darkening sky, desperately trying to distract herself from the brooding thoughts that invaded her consciousness. But those would not be denied.

Stuttern' Stuart!

She recoiled from the words that flashed through her senses as if she had been struck a blow.

Then she felt the tears start again. "Damn!" she said, angrily wiping her eyes on her sleeve. "D . . . damn!" She slumped to the grass shaking her head in resignation. I shouldn't have hit the little four–eyed, freckle–faced shithead. She silently reprimanded herself as she had been doing for the past several hours. What has happened to me? I've never done anything like that before.

Katie lay huddled in the depression formed by the creek that flowed through the pasture. For many years this had been her "secret place" where she could be alone. Lying next to the creek, she couldn't be seen by her mother from the house or by anyone else in town. Today she wanted to hide from them all—crawl down into the soft earth with the worms and the bugs, never again to be seen by human beings.

Looking through her tears she could see a tiny ant crawling among the blades of grass, each a hundred–foot tall tree by ant measurement. She could imagine herself, small as the ant, lying under one of the towering green spires. And all around would be dozens more blocking the view of thousands—millions even—that stood beyond. Being a size, in this impenetrable forest, they could search forever and never find her.

She made an attempt to locate herself. Looking carefully around the base of each stalk directly beneath her eyes, she tried to spot the tiny figure wearing the microscopic blue blouse and yellow slacks, but she couldn't. There were just too many places to hide. She could never be found. She was safe.

The comfort derived from this knowledge was abruptly ended by the realization that she wasn't a minuscule creature hidden under the grass, but a massive, looming and very obvious giant lying on the forest, crushing thousands of trees—a giant who could easily be seen by her mother giant or any of the other giants who might come looking for her. Exposed and vulnerable she pressed closer to the grass, yearning for the shelter that her tree, a real tree, had once provided.

Until the previous fall there had been a single tree growing on the bank of the creek. The broad, leafy maple had given cover to her secret place all those years and the winged seedpods had delighted the young girl with their whirling descent. She tried to pretend that the tree still stood overhead, reaching out to shield and protect her, but to no avail. There was too much sky, too much openness. It wasn't necessary to look. She could feel it.

The tree was gone, though, and that was that. A wild windstorm one night had blown it over. Katie had wept for her old friend as she'd watched Bart pull it away with his tractor.

After that she rarely visited her secret place and then it was just to stand and gaze at the torn earth where the roots had been pulled out. It could never be the same again.

She had started coming to the tree as a little girl—a frustrated and unhappy little girl—the summer after second grade. Katie could not believe that only nine years had passed since then. Something was wrong with the calendar. It must have been longer than that. She'd been attending school, it seemed, since the beginning of time—all those terrible years.

The awful toll that had been extracted from her emotional resources by those years, had been partially compensated by hours spent in her secret place. As a child, she had played with her toys, living little girl fantasies. Later, when she could read, she'd lain on the soft grass under the tree experiencing the adventures found in books that had been checked out of the Smithfield library.

Her mother knew of her refuge, of course. Probably saw me waving at the airplane, Katie thought. Have to face the music sometime—can't hide here forever. She'll soon be calling for me to come inside. And then it'll start all over again—the lecturing or, worse yet, the silent treatment. A shudder swept through the unhappy girl.

God! I hate that! She could picture her mother during those periods, grim and unapproachable as a sphinx, acknowledging her daughter's existence with only the most necessary utterances given in a deadly polite, rigidly composed manner:

"Would you like to clean the mud off your shoes?"

"Pass the bread, please, after you've helped yourself."

"Are you ready for bed now or do you have studies?"

Katie lived through these times in frantic desperation to get back into her mother's good graces. In a near frenzy she would tear into the household chores—washing, dusting, mopping—all the while watching her mother for some small sign of approval, which came only after a considerable period of repentance.

As the twilight dimmed, Katie shivered, feeling the cool air on her bare arms. She sat up, pulled her knees against her chest and gazed at the mountains to the east. The highest peaks were still being illuminated by the sun's last rays. By watching carefully, she could make out the shadow line advancing up the bare rock face of "Ol' Flat Top". Bart had told her its name. This was a long, almost horizontal ridge, topping one of the mountains of the Wasatch Range which formed the eastern border of Utah's Cache Valley.

Stuttern' Stuart!

Katie shook her head violently trying to shake loose the thoughts. "I've g . . . got to stop th . . . think . . . ing about it," she whispered to herself.

Chapter 2

Looking back at the town, she saw lights in the windows of houses and barns. She remembered then that she should have been helping Bart Johnson with the chores and milking. "Damn!" she swore in disappointment, striking the ground with her fist. He's probably wondering what happened to me—worried, maybe, that I might be sick. She scolded herself silently. The only reason she ever stayed away, without letting him know beforehand, was an occasional illness.

Katie couldn't remember when she had started going over to the old barn, but every evening—"regular as clockwork," Bart would say—she had followed the worn path from her back door to the farmyard. The wire fence between the properties had been crushed to uselessness, years ago, at the point of her frequent crossing. A gate had finally been installed to accommodate the youngster and still keep in the stock.

At first she had come just to visit—to have someone to be with—but after a while she'd begun helping. Gradually she had taken a more active part in the work. With the farmer's patient guidance, she'd assumed her own chores: setting out grain or silage to bring the cows into the barn from the corral or pasture, carrying milk cans and milk buckets, forking hay down from the loft, feeding the pigs and calves. She'd been particularly delighted teaching each newborn calf to drink from a bucket, holding the tiny muzzle submerged in the warm milk with fingers inside the calf's mouth to encourage sucking. How quickly they'd learned although Katie feared that the little animals might suffocate before realizing they couldn't breathe with their faces buried in milk.

In later years she had begun milking—one cow, at first, and then two after her hands had developed the necessary strength.

Katie liked being with the farm animals and having the comfortable feeling that they depended upon her. She liked being with Bart even more and she knew he appreciated having her around for company. He was a big, robust man with a voice of startling volume. What's more, he enjoyed talking. He talked to the cows and the horses and the pigs if human companionship was lacking. His own animals had become accustomed to his bellow and hardly flinched at his outbursts. He had, however, been known to cause some minor stampedes among unfamiliar cattle and, more than once, spook a team of horses into jumping the traces.

The farmer and the girl were a good match. Katie was an ardent listener, although she was certain at, times, that her ears would fall off. Nevertheless, she endured simply to be with the man. With him she felt important— that she had a purpose for her life. He gave her a reason for living and a sense of value for which she was eternally grateful. Also, she was aware of the great affection he had for her. It was an affection he would have lavished on a daughter of his own, if he'd had one. Bart's wife, Sarah, a quiet, loving little woman who adored her burly husband, was barren. Mrs Johnson was grateful for the young girl next door who provided the desperately needed presence of children in their lives.

Bart treated Katie as he would a child of his own, giving her the love and discipline he felt she needed. He was careful to compensate her for the work she did, increasing her pay proportionally each year and in accordance with the tasks she performed. He paid her a dollar a week for her help in the barn after school and extra when she worked all day Saturday. During the past summer she had been paid seventy-five cents a day for hoeing corn, beets and potatoes.

Bart never allowed her to do evening chores on those days when she worked in the fields, with one exception: He had left a wagon load of pea vines at the vinery awaiting his turn for unloading and driven his tractor to the field where she was hoeing corn. He'd asked if she would get started with the barn chores until he could get the wagon unloaded.

Katie had ridden back to the farmyard with him on the tractor, sitting in her usual place on the fender over one of the big wheels. Before he returned from the vinery, she had shoveled out the manure from the cow stalls and the calf pen, scattered in fresh straw, fed the pigs and chickens, put grain in the manger and herded the cows in from the pasture. She'd been ready to drop from exhaustion by the time Bart arrived but, nevertheless, proud to show what had been accomplished.

"No more of that!" her mother had declared. "Are you trying to kill yourself?"

But she had been paid a whole dollar and a half for just one very long day's work.

In addition to the money Bart paid her for working, there were the gifts. Christmas always brought something special and the wrist watch she wore—her most treasured possession—had been given her by the Johnsons on her fourteenth birthday.

She looked at the watch as she sat on the grass in her secret place. Too late, she thought. He's probably done by now. At that moment she saw the barn windows go dark and heard the familiar sound of the barn door closing.

"Damn!" she swore again,

Then she could hear him. He was talking to his dog in the high-pitched, irregular cadence manner of speaking that characterized the farmers in that area. Every word penetrated the calm evening air with remarkable clarity.

"God dammit, Duke, you ol' son of a bitch, watcha got there?"

Katie knew that he was totally incapable of expression without using "bad language". Her mother thought he was coarse and vulgar but then she really didn't know the man inside that boisterous exterior.

"Lemme see. Oh, so that's it! Now you want to play, you lazy bastard."

Katie could picture the big mongrel, rump and tail lifted, forelegs spread on the ground and a dilapidated rubber ball lying between its paws. With bright eagerness, the dog would be watching the big man approach—waiting for the game to start,

"You ain't done a lick all day. No wonder your so fulla' piss'n vinegar."

Duke, punctuating each of Bart's statements with yelps of joy, would be bouncing from side to side, pivoting about the ball.

"Alright, you simple shit, you wanna bust your ass, the least I can do is help you."

The dog's one sharp bark, a report that echoed among the surrounding buildings, signaled that he was off and running as his master was reaching for the ball.

Katie could visualize the animal's powerful back legs pumping in unison, claws tearing up pieces of sod as he gained astonishing speed toward the pasture. A mighty lunge and the dog popped into her view, clearing the five–foot high gate. At that moment, the ball came arcing over the pasture and Duke adjusted his velocity and direction to match its trajectory. A leap, a snap of jaws and he had the ball plucked neatly out of the air. Then back over the gate he soared, like an antelope, to drop the ball at Bart's feet.

"You stupid son of a bitch!" she heard him yell. "One of these days you're gonna break your goddamn neck."

This routine would be repeated, with the big farmer roaring profanity, until the light faded completely or until his wife opened the back door and called him inside.

Katie smiled to herself. Bart's rough talk was in direct contrast to his gentle nature, and his affection for the long–legged, black and white dog was legend in the small community. Duke was his constant companion. To see one was to know the other couldn't be far away.

She'd seen anger in the man only one time. The Peterson boy had thrown a rock for Duke to catch. Several of the old dog's teeth were cracked and chipped from catching rocks tossed by unthinking youths in the neighborhood.

"You do that agin', I'm gonna kick your ass right up under your ears," Bart had told the boy in a surprisingly quiet tone of voice.

Of course the big farmer had immediately felt sorry for the berated youngster who stood trembling, stammering apologies. With a big hand he'd ruffled the boy's hair, patiently explaining the damage done to the dog's mouth by rocks.

Katie was brought out of her reverie by her mother calling.

"Oh God!" she muttered, rising reluctantly. "Here we go again."

Chapter 3

"Nine dollars!" Clara Stuart repeated to her daughter. "That kind of money doesn't grow on trees."

Katie squirmed on her chair in misery. I don't have to keep hearing nine dollars, she thought. I'll remember that forever.

"Missus Farnley told me that both lenses were broken and one ear piece was bent so bad the frame will probably have to be replaced. Where do you think the money is coming from? We've got to pay for those glasses, whether you know it or not. I would think you'd remember that a grade school teacher doesn't earn a fortune—certainly not enough to be buying someone else's glasses that get broken by her irresponsible daughter. How could you let yourself strike that child?"

Katie, her supper untouched, sat at the table in despair as she had for thirty-seven minutes. Another furtive glance at the clock and some mental arithmetic confirmed the fact. In that period of time she'd heard her mother saying (and often repeating): ". . . they were fortunate the girl hadn't gotten glass in her eyes . . . there's an awful welt on the girl's cheek . . . her mother is fit to be tied . . . her father will probably be coming to see me . . ." and then, of course ". . . I can't, for the life of me, understand how you could do such a thing."

"What in the world got into you, anyway?" the mother demanded. "I know she's a little bitch—I had her in my class—but she's only ten years old."

I want to tell you why it happened, Mother, Katie thought. I want to tell you about all the times I've heard it, but you won't let me. You just don't understand how I feel. Her lips tightened as she recalled the pinched up face of Cynthia Farnley, orange freckles under orange hair and green pig–eyes. She felt again the rage that had consumed her when the girl, teeth bared in a sneer, screamed those horrid words up into her face—"Stuttern' Stuart"—not once but three times, the last interrupted by a hard slap on the face that had knocked the little girl to the sidewalk.

Katie had heard, or imagined hearing, those words before—from behind her in the bus, whispered in class or from a group standing in the corridors or out in the school-yard—always accompanied by giggles and glances in her direction. On those occasions she'd maintained the appearance of not having heard, keeping her head turned away and pretending that her attention was elsewhere. She'd been determined not to give them the satisfaction of seeing the hurt in her. And the hurt was real, sometimes an actual pain that she could feel in the center of her stomach. The humiliation and anger she'd had to hide, were almost more that she could bear. She wanted to hurt them in turn—smash them, even kill them—for what they were doing to her.

And now the worst has happened, she thought. Now I've actually hit someone.

Katie realized she'd missed much of her mother's tirade. She must be on her twentieth, ". . . how could you do such a thing? . . ." by now, Katie calculated. If she only knew how it happened. If she understood how I feel, but she won't listen. She just keeps talking. The tears were beginning to form again.

I can talk as well as anybody . . . inside, she reminded herself. I can say anything that anyone else can say, when I'm not trying so hard.

In her secret place, Katie had talked to herself, end-lessly, telling herself stories and jokes out loud with very little stuttering, assuring herself that she did, indeed, possess the power of speech.

But why can't I talk to someone else, she'd asked herself repeatedly. Why don't my lips and tongue do what they're supposed to do?

It wasn't always like this, she remembered. When we lived in Garden City I could talk a lot better—and I had friends there.

Her thoughts drifted back to happier times in the little community on the other side of the mountains. She saw again the blue Bear Lake—recalled the feel of the white sand under her bare feet and the warm water near the shore where she'd played with her friends all summer long. They could wade out from shore until the gradually deepening water covered all except their upturned faces. Then, bouncing off the bottom on "tippie toes", each would try to go a little beyond the others. For some reason she thought of Jill, going out too far and of Don, taller and stronger than the rest, who had pulled her to safety.

And it was Don, gifted with natural coordination, who'd been the first to learn to swim and then teach the others. In one summer, all had progressed from an awkward dog paddle to the much more efficient crawl.

A picture of the little farm across the road from the lake formed before Katie's staring eyes. Her memory still held the vision of tilled fields reaching up the gentle western slope from the lake until stopped by the forest. She recalled the house and barn—brown, bare wood. There had been six cows, two horses and two calves. She'd called the calves Tina and Pet.

Her father had laughed and said, "that's their names, all right. How did you know?"

She tried to remember her father's face and, again, found she couldn't. Why did he have to die?

"Huh!" Katie blurted out. She suddenly became aware that her mother's ranting had taken on new character.

"You heard me," Clara told her daughter. "You're going to have to pay for those glasses. Maybe that way you'll be a little more careful about your behavior in the future."

Katie looked at her mother for the first time since she had entered the house. She'd never had nine dollars all at the same time in her entire life and her mother knew it. The money she earned from Bart seemed to evaporate in a very short time. She saw every movie that came to Smithfield's two theaters—sometimes more than once. Then, of course, there were the ice cream and candy treats, magazines, trinkets for her room, an occasional tire for the bicycle, school supplies, incidental articles of clothing, some of this and some of that until the money was gone. Without the need to count, she knew that her immediate total bankroll was thirty-eight cents.

"Bart Johnson." Clara answered the question in her daughter's eyes. "I can't, for the life of me, understand why you want to hang around that smelly old barn of his, but he reminded me again of what a good worker you are and wondered if you'd be interested in something besides hoeing this summer."

Katie frowned and opened her mouth to speak but her mother continued, impatiently. "I saw him in Griffith's store last week. He asked me . . ." Clara broke off, her face registering displeasure. "God! He asked everyone in the county with that voice of his. He asked if it would be all right for you to try thinning beets for him when school's out. I didn't think you'd want to—that's brutal work—but I told him I'd mention it to you. Now I think it's a good idea. Maybe it'll teach you a thing or two."

As Clara turned away to the sink, her daughter watched, unbelieving. She had always been discouraged by her mother from doing farm work, even on the church farm with the other kids. This disturbed the young girl. Katie enjoyed the out–of–doors activity. The hot sun felt good on her skin. She had welcomed the exercise and the sense of accomplishment when she'd hoed four rows of potatoes at a time.

Of course, she had been always aware of her mother's distaste for farm life. Among her earliest recollections was hearing the constant complaints about the dirt, the flies, the smell and the hard work.

Bart had explained why this was so. "It's hard on a woman that ain't been born to it. Those that have don't know nothin' better."

Aware of how her mother felt about farm life, Katie often wondered why a college girl from Salt Lake City came to marry a farmer. Her mother had never talked about it but the young girl had pestered her Grandma Collins again and again to tell about her mother having fallen in love with Frank Stuart while visiting a school friend at Bear Lake. The visit had lasted most of the summer with Clara Collins spending as much time with her new beau as he could spare away from his farm. Occasionally she'd gone into the fields and watched him work. As he'd labored—loading hay, cleaning ditches or hoeing potatoes—he'd talked earnestly about his plans for the little farm: paying off the mortgage, building a new barn and acquiring more dairy cows.

After the youthful college men she had known, Frank had seemed even more mature than his twenty-five years would account for and more manly. With his tall, rangy form, wide-set blue eyes and strong jaw line, he'd been the epitome of maleness to the young woman. The intensity of her attraction to him had been surprising and somewhat frightening to Clara.

When she'd returned to Salt Lake City with her young man in tow and announced that they would marry the following spring after her graduation, Fred Collins had been appalled that his educated daughter was throwing away her life on a farmer who hadn't even finished high school. He'd no chance, however, against the two headstrong women in his household. His argument, that Clara didn't have any idea about the life she was letting herself in for, had fallen on deaf ears. The wedding had taken place as planned.

Clara had endured the farm life purely out of love for her husband. She was too stubborn to ever admit to her parents that she wasn't entirely happy with her life, although it had been a meager existence, indeed. The young family had survived in a state of near poverty. There had been food, to be sure, but hardly any money for the purchase of normal necessities. Almost everything the little farm produced had gone into paying the interest on the mortgage. Rarely had any extra been available to be applied to the principle.

Clara had made clothes for herself, Frank and, after Katie arrived, for her daughter. Several times a year, Fred and Martha had driven up to Bear Lake for a visit—more frequently after their granddaughter had been born. They always brought a car full of materials and articles that Mother Collins had carefully declared were "extras" or "not much good but maybe can be put to some use."

Upon leaving, Fred would press a ten dollar bill into his daughter's hand saying that it was a birthday gift. So desperate had been their need that Clara couldn't bring herself to remind him that she had a birthday only once a year like everyone else.

Frank had accepted the generosity of his wife's parents the same as he accepted Fred's feigned interest in the operation of the farm—with resigned good nature. As partial compensation, he made it a policy to send them home with some items of food: a sack of potatoes, a leg of venison or antelope, several pounds of freshly churned butter. Clara usually added a few jars of homemade strawberry or raspberry preserves.

Katie remembered how she'd looked forward to the visits of grandma and grandpa Collins. They'd always brought gifts—one time a puppy she'd named Pepper. Other times, nice clothes and a toy or game. Grandpa always played the games with her.

If her family suffered hardships, Katie had been unaware of the fact. There had always been enough of everything for her. She loved the farm and the animals, the open space in which to run wild, the lake in the summer, the snow in the winter, the anticipation of Christmas, Easter, and her birthday.

Even after her father died from being kicked in the head by Ol' Jake while hitching the horse to a hay rake, Katie had never realized how serious their plight. Her mother had begun teaching school full time whereas she'd only "helped out" before. The operation of the farm was taken over by Uncle Al. Everything else had seemed much the same except that she missed her father terribly and her mother never seemed happy anymore.

Katie was, again, jarred back to reality by her mother's voice.

"Tell Bart you can start when school is out," Clara stated with finality.

* * *

The following evening Katie worked in the barn with Bart. She cleaned the calf pen while he shoveled manure out of the gutter into a wheelbarrow. Straw was then scattered on the platform next to the stanchions and in the calf pen.

Katie emptied a pan full of grain in front of each cow stall while Bart called in the cows from the pasture. Each hurried to its respective stall and started eating the grain. Katie squeezed in between cows and locked the stanchions. Afterwards she washed the cow's udders and Bart started hand-milking the cows.

Katie fed a newborn calf with milk from a bucket and then used a pitchfork to fill the manger with hay. She milked one of the last cows so that she and Bart finished at the same time.

"That's another day." Bart winked at Katie. He placed a lid on the milk can and carried it outside. When he returned he looked at the girl. "I heard what happened. Somebody told me you slapped Cynthia Farnley and broke her glasses."

Katie stood in front of the big farmer with her head hanging.

"Now that doesn't sound like you. Do you want to tell me about it?"

Tears began flowing down Katie's cheeks and she made a moaning sound. Bart took her in his arms and patted her on the back as she continued to sob. "There, there. It can't be all that bad."

"She c . . . call . . . called m . . . me . . .," Katie began in a muffled voice.

"There, there. I know. She called you Stuttern' Stuart."

A muffled wail came from Katie as she clung to the farmer.

The big man's voice was surprisingly quiet. I can only guess how you feel," he said. "You've got a lot of personal pride and to think that you're known only as someone who stutters, hurts like nothing else can."

He kissed her on the top of her head. "But I know there's more to you than that. There's a lot more to you than there is to most folks, and deep inside, you know it too. That's what hurts so much because you can't bring it out. But you will, someday. You will. Take my word for it."

Chapter 4

"Here comes muscles!"

Katie felt her face flaming as she boarded the school bus the following Monday morning. She had dreaded this moment the entire weekend and now it had arrived. She sat quickly in the first empty seat next to Sally Peterson.

"Look out for her, Sally," someone shouted from the back of the bus. "She's hell on little kids."

This provoked a burst of laughter behind Katie. The tenth grade girl next to her, small for her age, sat tight–lipped, staring straight ahead.

Katie had purposely avoided, until the last minute, the group that waited in front of Summit grade school for the bus that delivered the older students to the high school in Richmond. Now her worst fears were confirmed.

They all know, she thought, mortified. The whole town knows—probably everyone in Cache County.

The seven mile ride to North Cache High seemed to take forever. Each whisper, each giggle Katie felt was directed at her. She could sense their eyes, their pointing fingers, their smirks.

Stuttern' Stuart knocked Cynthia Farnley down and broke her glasses, she could almost hear them saying. Stuttern' Stuart did it! Stuttern' Stuart!

Shitheads! She grew more resentful and agitated with every creeping mile. By the time the school came into view, Katie could feel the familiar trembling start in her arms and legs. She rushed into the building, grateful that none of those on the bus were in her first class.

Later, walking out of the classroom with her head down, she collided with Dwaine Parkins.

"Whoa!" he said grasping her shoulders. "Steady there, girl."

"They jes' keep throwin' theirselves at ya, don't they buddy? Hee hee hee!" Will Fletcher, with his characteristic soprano giggle, was standing next to his friend.

"You okay, Katie?" The concerned look on Dwaine's face told the embarrassed girl that he knew about Cynthia.

Her answer was a wan smile and a slight shrug.

"Don't let 'em get to you." He walked beside her, patting her on the back. "The little hellion had it coming."

"That's for damn sure!" Will agreed.

Will was one year ahead of her in school—a big, good–natured farm boy. His clown face wore a perpetual grin and his congeniality was infectious. Whenever a crowd had gathered on the school grounds, laughing and joking, Will was invariably at its center. In spite of her best efforts to remain straight–faced, Katie had caught herself giggling at some of his antics and outbursts.

If the girls thought Will was "cute" it was his friend that captured most of their attention. Dwaine had graduated the previous year. He had been, however, a familiar figure around North Cache High in the past year. Having won his letters in football, basketball and track, he'd retained an intense interest in the school sports and attended nearly every event.

His friendship with the coach had continued and, as a former captain of the football team, his observations at training and practice sessions were welcomed.

It was through football that he and Will had become fast friends. The two contrasted strangely—Will's bulk and Dwaine's muscular lean form, Will's brash manner and Dwaine's quiet, soft–spoken nature. Yet they complimented each other. Dwaine, who showed great appreciation for his pal's humor, was also an able parry for his friend's sharp thrusts of wit. Will, on the other hand, relied heavily on the older youth's sense of direction—his purposefulness.

The two enjoyed many common interests, in addition to school sports—hunting, fishing, horses and, of course, girls. Will's admiration for the other's success with the young ladies in the valley, knew no bounds.

Katie, along with the other girls, had followed him, surreptitiously, with their eyes as he roamed about the school. At somewhat over six–feet tall, he carried a disproportionate amount of himself in chest and arms.

Katie had been most impressed by the easy manner he showed moving through the school society—a pat on the back, a casual arm over a shoulder and a carefully cultivated, bashful grin that the girls found irresistible. He seemed to know and take an interest in everyone—even a shy girl with a stutter. The first time he spoke to her, Katie had been shocked that he even knew her name.

She had watched as the girls performed for him: bright red smiles, arched eyebrows, shoulders back, posing, prancing, purring, giggling.

I would never do that, she assured herself.

When Dwaine and Will had driven away from the school in Dwaine's Pontiac coupe, more often than not several of North Cache High's prettiest young ladies accompanied them—Will sitting in the rumble seat with one or two, and another alongside the driver.

Walking between Will and Dwaine in the corridor, Katie couldn't help but notice the questioning glances she received.

They're wondering if I'm one of Dwaine's girls, she thought.

Will's voice broke into her thoughts. "Better get goin', ol' buddy. Coach wants to see you. Probably goin' to ask if you can help out again next year."

Although grateful for their support, Katie was immensely relieved when the two boys departed. She had felt uncomfortable with Dwaine so close—particularly conscious of the interest being shown her by the other girls. Equally disturbing was her inability to contribute to the conversation carried on amicably by the young men.

Somehow she managed to get through the rest of the day, although she couldn't recall having experienced a worse time. And then, to make matters worse, Billy caught up with her in the hall.

"*K-K-K-Katie . . .*"

He sang a song that had been popular years before:

"*Beautiful Katie. You're the only g-g-g-girl that I adore.*"

Katie glared at the youth, also a junior and the school cutup who teased her constantly. She hated that song about a girl named Katie who stuttered.

"*When the m-m-moon shines over the c-cow shed,*
I'll be waiting for you at the k-k-kitchen door."

He laughed with a group of nearby students and danced around her in a fighter's stance. "I hear you've got a pretty good right cross," he said. "How's your uppercut?"

Katie started to walk away, but Billie followed. "Did you hear about the girl who talked so slow that before she could say she wasn't that kinda' girl, she was that kinda' girl." More laughter followed.

Katie stopped and turned angrily on the youth, who was almost a head shorter. "Oops," he said. "Better go."

Most of the jibes, directed at her by classmates, were in the form of jokes. Even when the hazing became rather intense—although still in fun—Katie managed to maintain her composure. But there was no humor involved in the one incident that caused her to break down into uncontrollable sobbing and left her an emotional wreck the rest of the day. That happened during the lunch period.

She was sitting outside on the grass, apart from the general congregation of students, as usual. Her sandwich lay uneaten from lack of appetite and she was gnawing, without enthusiasm, on an apple while reviewing geometry problems. The final examination was scheduled for that afternoon. The last thing on her mind was Mel Farnley until he announced his presence by kicking the book out of her hand.

"You hit m' lil' sister," he blurted out. "Somebody oughta hit you! Bitch!"

Mel would have to be described, even in the kindest terms, as loutish. At nineteen, he was only a sophomore having been held back two years in grade school. Totally incapable of higher levels of learning, teachers had advanced him in grade simply to avoid having him repeat their classes. He was a bully and a troublemaker. Squat and stocky in stature, he was brute-strong from years of farm labor. The school's football coach made good use of his aggressive nature, playing him in a guard position on the line. He seemed oblivious to pain and thrived on contact to the degree that opposing team players were quickly intimidated by the fury of his attacks. Members of his own team, with few exceptions, carefully avoided any confrontation with him.

As if his behavior wasn't sufficiently threatening, his appearance compounded the total effect. He was unbecoming in every way. A broad brow hung precipitously over little green eyes, a blunt nose, protruding lips and almost no chin at all. This countenance was peppered with rust—colored freckles and topped by a thatch of carrot—red hair that lacked any form of discipline.

If he had ever practiced personal hygiene, it was infrequent and of limited exposure. His teeth were black with rot and he reeked to the extent that those forced to pass him in close proximity, chose to forego the luxury of breathing.

Katie's hand was numb from the kick as was her brain from his sudden, violent appearance. She could only stare at him with wide eyes. When he bent over her, his face only inches from hers, she almost gagged from the stench.

"Bitch! Why don'tcha' hit me? Then see whatcha' git."

A crowd, always eager for excitement, soon gathered about the two.

"Go on! Hit me, bitch! Hit me! Hit me! Bitch! Bitch! Bitch!" With his hand raised ominously, ready to deliver an answering blow, he rained a torrent of spittle and unimaginative verbal abuse on the terrified girl.

Katie, sick from the attention that was being drawn to her almost as much as from fright, burst into tears.

"Mel!" A voice came from behind the group of onlookers. "Leave her alone. I'm only going to tell you once."

By the time Katie could dry her eyes and collect herself, she saw only the broad back of her assailant as he stomped away. The spectators were also leaving—disappointed.

She didn't learn, until a long time afterwards, that it was Dwaine Parkins who came to her rescue.

Chapter 5

"Well now, Sir Galihad," Will said to his friend, "I didn't know you was a defender of ladies in distress. That may not have been a good idee takin' on Mel. You'd better watch out for him. He's a mean son of a bitch."

"You've got that right, "Dwaine said.

They walked into the locker room.

"I wouldn't want to tangle with him over any gal," Will said, "but why Stutterin' Stuart?"

"Hell, Will. I couldn't very well stand there and watch him beat up on a girl—any girl. Somebody had to get him out of there."

"That's right. You've got to protect your own private harem." Will laughed along with a number of other young men standing nearby. "So who will be the next one?"

Dwaine grinned. "Next what?"

"You know damn well next what!" Will's statement was accompanied by more laughter. "I saw you talking with Rosie a while ago. What do you think of her?"

"Cute kid."

"It looked like she wanted to climb all over you," the big youth said. "Could you go for some of that?"

"Too young," Dwaine said.

"Too young?" Will's expression was one of disbelief. "What do you mean too young? She's a sophomore. Never bothered you before. If they're big enough they're old enough."

A larger group of young men gathered about the pair as they engaged in their typical banter. Two had emerged from the shower room and stood dripping water. All were laughing with Will.

"If it's not her, then who?"

Dwaine laughed. "No one. You know I don't go in for that stuff."

Will rolled his eyes. "No, of course not. That's why there won't be a virgin left in the school before you're done. Come on, Dwaine! There are hundreds of girls in North Cache, thousand in Utah, millions in the country and in the world . . ." Will threw his big arms wide and let them drop helplessly. "My God, Dwaine! You can't make 'em all."

Dwaine laughed with everyone else and shook his head. "Knock it off."

Will turned to the young men standing nearby. "Do you know why Elmer's always asleep in class? Dwaine's payin' him to do his sleeping so he won't waste any time." The locker room exploded in laughter. Will giggled as Dwaine balled a fist and pounded his friend's upper arm.

"How come you get all the gals?" Will wanted to know. "What've you got I ain't got?"

"Simple," the other replied. "You're ugly as a toad and I'm a handsome devil."

At that moment Mel Farnley came into the locker room. The young men parted apprehensively as he walked directly to Dwaine. He stood for a moment and then abruptly shoved the taller man against the wall. Quicker than Mel could react, Dwaine unleashed a rapid barrage of punches that put Mel on the floor, unconscious.

Coach Pete Connelly hurried in from his office. "What the hell's going on here?" He looked down at the prone figure of Mel. "What happened to him?"

The men standing around looked nervously at each other.

"He slipped," Will said.

"Yeah," the others said in unison, "he slipped."

The coach looked at each of the young men in turn and then at Dwaine. He noted he skinned knuckles. "I can see that," he said. "Floor's wet. Of course he slipped. You two," he pointed to two of the bigger men, "help me get him into the office so I can bring him around."

Everyone stood watching as the three carried Mel away. "Better get something to put on them knuckles," Will told his friend."

Dwaine nodded.

Burke Nolan, a big football player stood next to Will as Dwaine walked away. "I ain't never saw nothin' like that before. Mel didn't have time to lift his hands."

"You don't ever want to go mixin' it up with Dwaine," Will told the other. "He got that build flippin' around grain sacks in his old man's feed store. He's got muscles where there shouldn't be muscles."

Burke shook his head. "First time I ever seen him real mad either."

"Better make sure it's the last time," Will said, "'specially if it's you he's mad at."

Chapter 6

The remainder of the week wasn't as bad for her as she had dreaded. There were the final exams, of course, but these didn't bother her too much. She was a good student and she applied herself to her studies, since she had so few distractions of a social nature. A real blessing was the extracurricular activities—the assemblies, the school play, the concert, the track and field events—of the final week that reduced the time Katie had to spend in the classroom. There she lived in constant fear that she would be called upon by teachers to speak.

When she started third grade at Summit, she had made a real effort to answer when the teacher asked questions. The kids in her classes, when she had lived in Garden City, were accustomed to her halting speech and paid little attention. They were her friends. There was none of the laughter, the giggles, the taunts and mimicking of her stutter, that she experienced at Summit.

After a while it seemed easier not to talk at all than to endure the ridicule.

School, she would remember always, was the worst time of her life. She wished it was over and done with for good but, at the same time, she was relieved that she didn't have to walk out on the stage in front of everyone to receive a diploma. How she could bring herself to face the graduation exercises next year, she had no idea.

Maybe I won't live until nineteen thirty-nine, she thought with certain optimism.

* * *

Katie sat in front of the school waiting for the school bus that would take the students to Smithfield. She saw Dwaine and Will drive up and stop next to several girls standing near the street. The girls were laughing as Will talked.

Seated a short distance away from Katie were three girls. The one named Opal was a classmate of Katie's. The other two, Georgina and Della, were seniors. They had been chatting, but grew quiet and watched, from their remote vantage point, as the Pontiac stopped.

"Will's probably telling another of his dirty jokes," Georgina said. "Wonder which one it is this time."

"Oh!" Della looked at her friend. "You've heard all his dirty jokes?"

"No, not all, but I know they're all dirty and he doesn't care who hears them."

"These jokes wouldn't have anything to do with sex, would they?" Della showed Georgina a wry expression. "I can't imagine how he'd know anything about sex just by hanging around with Dwaine." The two girls laughed.

Opal scowled. "I don't believe all that stuff they say about Dwaine. People make up stuff. I think he's kinda' cute.

Della's eyebrows lifted. "Cute? How?"

"Well ... sorta' good-looking. You know, handsome."

Della laughed. "How's that?"

"Well he looks a little bit like Douglas Fairbanks." Opal giggled. "Don't tell me you haven't noticed. I've seen you looking at him."

"Now what was I supposed to notice about him?"

"That he's sorta' debonair—aristocratic," Opal said.

"Aristocratic! Oh sure! You've got stars in your eyes, girl." Della showed the younger girl an expression of contempt. "I suppose you'd like to cozy up to ol' Dwaine yourself. Didn't you hear that Marcy said he still had her panties?"

Della noticed Katie's head turned slightly to listen to the conversation and smiled.

"Well," Opal said peevishly, "that don't mean they went all the way. They could have just been making out a little."

"A little! She said he didn't use a rubber—scared as hell she might get knocked up"

"When did you hear that?"

"I heard her telling Shelly," Della said. "Everybody knows Shelly has been putting out for Dwaine since she was a sophomore."

"Shelly is a slut," Georgina broke into the conversation. "She's been putting out for all the guys in school—anything that wears pants."

"Oh oh!" Della said. "Looks like Dwaine and Will have got some takers."

Katie looked up to see Will opening the car's rumble seat.

"Who's going with them this time?"

"That's Susan getting in front with Dwaine," Georgina said. "I thought she was such a goodie goodie girl."

"And it's that tramp, Zelma, getting in back with Will," Della added. "Will's gonna' have his hands full before long."

Georgina giggled. "Della! That's awful."

"You're both awful." Opal said.

Della gave the younger girl a pointed look. "One thing for certain—anybody going off with that pair is going to have their reputation shot in this school."

"Yeah," Opal said wistfully.

"Sounds to me like you'd like to give ol' Dwaine a ride yourself," Della told the younger girl. "That's easy enough to arrange. Just rub your tits up against him sometime and you'll have your chance."

Katie blushed with embarrassment. She quickly gathered her school supplies and hurried away. Della and Georgina laughed at her departure.

"You're both awful," Opal said again.

Chapter 7

Her back ached. The muscles seemed on fire. Bart had said it would hurt for a while. Now, after the sixth day, Katie wondered how much longer it would take to become accustomed to the awkward position so that the pain would subside. Bent at the waist, her legs straddled two rows of sprouting sugar beet plants.

She straightened upright, rubbed her back with the knuckles of her free hand and checked, again, to see how far she had come. It seemed hardly any distance at all since the last time she looked. After she examined the stub–handled hoe and verifed it could wait for sharpening until the end of the row, she bent doggedly to her task.

One or two slashes with the hoe isolated a small cluster of plants, which was then hand-picked leaving one plant—the biggest, hardiest. The routine had quickly become second nature, performed without conscious thought, so that her mind was free to dwell on a variety of subjects. That helped take her attention away from her discomfort.

She remembered books she had read, movies she had seen and she lived the stories again in her mind. Casting herself in the principal female roles, she was Maid Marian being rescued by a dashing Robin Hood, Dale exploring the universe with Flash Gordon, Ginger Rodgers dancing with Fred Astaire, Jeanette MacDonald singing with Nelson Eddy.

That morning, invigorated by the fresh air, she sang her favorite songs, making up lyrics for those she didn't know:

"Heartaches, heartaches.
My loving you meant only heartaches.
I should be happy with someone new,
But my heart aches for you."

She never stuttered when she sang and couldn't understand the reason for that. Maybe instead of talking, I should sing what I want to say, she considered, and began singing:

> *"Heartaches, backaches . . ."*

Katie paused thinking of other lyrics for the Hoffman/Klen song.

> *"It won't be long before my back breaks."*

Another pause . . .

> *"Bart Johnson told me it would not last long . . .*
> *I didn't know that he could be so wrong . . ."*

She paused again—this time longer.

> *"Arm pain, neck pain . . . if this gets*
> *worse I know I'll go insane . . ."*

Pause:

> *"If he was here now I know what I'd do,*
> *I'd hit him on the head with his goddamn hoe."*

Katie dropped to her knees laughing. Now I'm getting silly, she thought.

Standing, she bent once more over the beet plants. What am I doing here? This isn't where a refined young woman like me should be, she thought. I shouldn't be working like a common peasant. Anyone would know just by looking at me that I'm really a princess of old European royalty who has been brought to America by the Queen in exile—my mother. Queen Clara. Or, maybe she isn't really my mother. Maybe I was kidnapped and someday they'll find me working in these fields. Then I'll be returned in glorious triumph to the land of my birth and to my adoring subjects where I'll live in splendor the rest of my life.

Or maybe, she thought, I'm a French princess like Jeanette Macdonald in "Naughty Marietta" and I'll be falling in love with Nelson Eddy, the Indian scout.

Katie stood and, hoe on shoulder, began marching and singing the Herbert/Young song:

> *"Tramp tramp tramp along the highway,*
> *Tramp tramp tramp the road is free.*
> *Blazing trails along the byway,*
> *soldiers . . .the something . . . are we.*
> *Tramp tramp tramp now clear the roadway,*

Room room room the world is free.
We're planters and . . . something ducks,
Virginians and . . ."

Katie suddenly stopped marching and quickly looked around. Somebody might think I'm crazy, she thought, as she started to work again. I wonder if this princess will ever find her Indian scout. Will the Indian scout love me?

She began to sing softly, as she worked, the Kern/Hammerstein song from Showboat:

"We could make believe I love you.
We could make believe that you love me.
Might as well make believe . . ."

That's probably all I'll ever do is make believe, she thought. I could never do what those other girls do to get the attention of boys—certainly not what Della told Opal. I'd die if the kids thought I was like Shelly—one of Dwaine's girls. I don't need that kind of reputation. I've already got a reputation as a stutterer who hits little kids. Now here I am working my ass off to buy new glasses for that little shithead.

But I've just got to stop thinking about it.

"Stop, stop, stop," she said aloud. Think of something else, she counseled herself silently. As she worked, she forced her mind into creating scenarios, taken from bits and pieces of the many movies she'd seen or books she'd read and imagined herself in soul-stirring situations. She was the tragic heroine who, in saving the handsome man from certain death, almost loses her own life. Tears flowed, uninhibited, down her cheeks as she visualized herself lying, pale and still on the hospital bed while nearby, the remorseful young fellow—he looked remarkably like Tyrone Power—begged her to live so he could devote his life to her.

Other times she thought about love. Having never received serious attention from a boy, she was more than a little curious—wondered what it would be like. She yearned for the real experiences some of the girls at school talked about with knowing looks and giggles. The ease with which they conducted themselves in the company of the young men was a source of envy to Katie. How she hungered to be like them. Many times she had stood before the mirror in her room trying to duplicate their expressions—arching an eyebrow, lifting one side of her mouth, tilting her head.

How effortlessly those girls could tell others of their thoughts and feelings. She had watched, covertly, trying to understand their conversations, the innuendoes, the subtle signals that were exchanged. She wondered about the suggestive remarks made by the boys, accompanied by winks and leers—the words she recognized but the meaning often escaped her. Sometimes she didn't even understand the words.

Comments made by some of the girls, in voices subdued so that Katie had to listen with rapt attention, hinted at liaisons of such intimacy that she would be forced to flee least her flaming face give her away.

Later, in the safety of her room, she would ponder the implication of what she had overheard. With only a vague notion of what was meant by "going all the way" or "making-out", this speculation did nothing more than add to her curiosity and confusion.

The girls who enjoyed the most attention from the young men at North Cache High, were those who seemed to be walking a thin line between unspoken promise and acquiescence. Shelly was one who had, obviously, stepped over to the wrong side of the line.

Katie thought of her with a mixture of pity and disgust. The girl, whose figure had ripened early into voluptuousness, had gained the reputation of being "easy"—whether justified or not—and found herself the target of crude remarks and obscene gestures from the boys and sneers from the girls. Katie could sympathize with Shelly's desperate desire to establish friendships among the other students— even someone who stuttered—but was repulsed by the girl's ingratiating overtures.

That day, in the field, she was in a melancholy mood. The realization that she was working a full week and part of next week as the result of one sudden reflex action, caused her spirits to sink to new depths. On several occasions, as her weariness grew, she found herself crying.

Other times she fumed silently. Dumb little shithead! I shouldn't have hit her. Why did she yell that name right into my face. I've never done anything to her—don't hardly know the little shithead. Besides, Katie reasoned, it couldn't have been her idea. She hasn't got brains enough to come up with that name on her own. Somebody put her up to it.

A mental image of the scene formed before her eyes. She could almost picture someone of the high school group that still remained on the Summit school grounds—someone who had been on the bus returning from North Cache. No specific face could be identified but that person had, undoubtedly, told the child, "Go call Katie 'Stuttern' Stuart'. Go on! I dare you!"

Big joke. Real funny.

Stuttern' Stuart. That dreadful name rang in her ears. At times she could almost forget, but it was always there— lurking in some dark recess of her consciousness—ready to spring out to shock her, bringing forth another flow of tears.

I've got to stop thinking about it, she told herself again and again. But, still her thoughts flew, uncontrolled, back to the playground at Summit school—to the girl sprawled on the cement, screaming with rage and pain. When Katie remembered the scream, her legs and arms would begin to tremble, like before, when she'd stood over the youngster—not able to move, not able to think—staring at her.

She had a vague recollection of the crowd of children gathered around, of Missus Ames saying repeatedly, "What happened?" And of the bus driver, Mister Hanson, lifting the girl from the ground.

Missus Ames, after listening to recounts of the inci- dent, supplied in glowing detail by a number of eager observers, had sent one of her third-grade students to see if "Missus Stuart was still in the school building." It had been the mention of her mother's name that had caused Katie to recover her wits.

Her scramble for the bicycle and her frantic pedaling away from the nightmare scene had been accompanied by Missus Ames's angry shouting, "You come back here, Katie. Your mother's going to hear about this!"

Bent over the rows of beet plants, Katie watched her tears making brown dots on the sun-bleached clods of dirt. I've got to stop thinking about it, she reminded herself.

It was at that moment she heard the airplane again.

Chapter 8

He was cleaning the oil drain pan when he saw her coming along the road from Benson Ward. Skinny kid, he noted absently. She was standing on the bicycle's pedals, strong legs thrusting to overcome the reluctance of balloon tires to roll on the graveled surface.

On her way to Loganna, he decided. Long way to ride for a swim.

Carrying the pan and funnel, he walked into the crude shed that served to shelter the airplane. He liked to think of it as "the hangar" and laughed at himself for this presumption. With others he referred to it as "the barn". He had built the structure from rough lumber, using tar paper to cover the roof boards. Some day he meant to put shingles or, maybe, corrugated steel over the tar paper.

After storing the utensils under the corner workbench, he wiped his hands on some cotton waste and walked into the tiny office he'd partitioned off in a back corner of the building.

Twenty-five hours sure goes by in a hurry, he mused as he recorded the oil change in the log book. In just that little time, the oil still comes out quite dark. But then air-cooled engines run hotter.

He hunched over the desk scrawling in the little book, a stocky man in his mid forties. The precise manner in which he recorded each distinct character gave evidence of the meticulous attention he applied to every detail in his life.

She was standing, looking at the airplane, when he stepped out of the building, unnoticed, behind her. He watched as she tentatively touched the fabric on the wing. The fat little tire captured her interest for a moment, then she turned her attention to the open doors on the side. Ducking under the wing, she grasped a strut for support. When the airplane shifted slightly, she quickly pulled her hand away and stepped back. Her eyes wandered over the craft, taking in the gleaming wooden propeller, the cowling that covered the engine, the Plexiglas windows, the tapering body, the wings and other protruding surfaces. Finally she moved in close to examine the interior.

"It's a Piper Cub." He was immediately sorry that he hadn't made his presence known more gently. Her entire form jerked at the sound of his voice and her head bumped against the underside of the wing. But still, at the same time, he had to laugh at her reaction. She grinned sheepishly, rubbing her head.

"They usually let me out on Halloween to scare the young ladies but I think they're a little early this year."

He saw the tension go out of her, then, and the color return to her face. "Hiya, I'm Crow, Crowther Spencer actually, but everyone calls me Crow." he was trying to put her at ease. "Seen one of these before?" He indicated the airplane.

She shook her head, smiling.

No ravishing beauty, he thought, but a smile that lights up the world. Sensing her nervousness, he began making a cigarette—tissue paper fished out of the pack, Bull Durham poured from the cloth pouch, rolled, wetted and sealed. "You live around here?" he said before lighting.

She nodded toward the north end of the valley.

"Smithfield, eh? That's quite a ride. On your way to Loganna?"

She shook her head and grinned, embarrassed.

"Oh yeah. I see," he said chuckling. "Came to see the plane. All that way, huh? That's okay. A lot of the kids drop by for a look. What's your name?"

The steady gaze, with which she had regarded him, suddenly faltered. With her head lowered, he could barely hear her speak. "K . . . K . . . Ka . . . Katie."

Oh no! he thought, his suspicions confirmed, Not a girl stutterer! Girls were born to talk and talk and talk. But he had recognized the signs: mouth open with lips extended, eyes fixed and staring, neck and jaw muscles rigid, head jerking and his heart went out to her.

"Well Katie," he went on smoothly while trying not to show his concern, let me tell you all about this here 'aer-ee-o-plane'." He wanted her to smile again.

"As I said before you tried to poke your head through the wing, it's a Piper Cub, model J-Three, built back east. Couple of months back, I took the train to Pennsylvania and picked it up. Took me almost a week to fly home, what with the winter weather and all. Besides, it's not the fastest plane made."

He paused to take a long drag on his cigarette and collect his thoughts. "Let's see now, it's got an engine that may develop fifty horsepower at this altitude, although I doubt it. Weighs a little over five-hundred pounds empty." He grinned at her. "Not very heavy, is it? I've heard that Ol' Man Piper can pick up one of these things—said he wouldn't build an airplane he couldn't lift. Might be true—he's a big cuss so I wouldn't be surprised. I met him while I was back there at Lockhaven."

She took hold of the wing strut and jiggled the airplane experimentally. Her smile returned.

I like her, he decided. She's got something special.

"It will carry two people, if they're not too big, twelve gallons of gas and hardly anything else. Goes a little over seventy miles an hour, climbs at about three-hundred feet per minute—less at higher altitude or on hot days—and will get up to the height of those mountains," he pointed to the east, "if you've got enough time."

He was enjoying himself. "Have I missed anything?"

She shrugged and, still smiling, began self-consciously studying the craft—touching, feeling the smooth yellow surfaces.

Her interest encouraged him to continue. "The structure is welded steel tubing in the fuselage." He pointed, in answer to her questioning look. "The body, that part with the seats inside. By the way, 'fuselage' is a French word. Means tapering. I don't know why someone decided to give airplane parts French names. Must have sounded more elegant."

"The wing has wood spars—structural beams—here and here." He showed with his hands. "The ribs that go across the wing, this way, give the wing its curved shape on top. The whole thing, then, is covered with a cotton fabric—something like bed sheets—and painted with a kind of cellulose material to make it tight and hard."

He watched as she walked along in a stoop under the wing, feeling the framework beneath the fabric. "I watched them being built at the factory. I guess it does away with the wonder of it all when you see how they're made and understand that they're just another machine. That's an aileron."

She had moved out near the end of the wing and noticed that the section along the back edge was hinged so that it moved up and down with her touch.

"Makes the plane bank—you know, tilt—in a turn," he said. "Roads are banked to keep cars from sliding off in a turn. There are no roads up there," he pointed skyward, "so we build the banks into the airplane." He showed her, with arms outstretched, walking in a circle.

She had to laugh at his antics.

He finished his cigarette in thoughtful silence, watching the girl as she resumed her examination of the plane. She moved the aileron again and caught sight of the control stick inside the plane moving in response. He saw her nod of comprehension. With the cigarette crushed out, he made up his mind. This girl should fly.

"I've got some spare time this morning if you'd like a quick course in aeronautics from professor C. J. Spencer."

He saw one eyebrow lift quizzically, so he performed a mock bow. "Straight from the school of hard knocks. Are you interested in knowing what makes this thing tick?" He gestured toward the airplane.

Not convinced that he was serious, she shrugged, uncertainly.

"Well?"

She shrugged again, but smiled.

Chapter 9

"All right. Let's start here in front."

She followed as he ducked under the wing and made his way forward.

"The propeller works just like an electric fan. Pushing the air back, the propeller wants to go forward and pull the plane with it."

He saw the questioning look in her eyes. "It's like swimming," he said. "Can you swim?"

She nodded.

"So, what do you do in order to swim? You grab the water in front of you and push it behind to make yourself go forward. Isn't that right?" He made exaggerated swimming movements.

Katie smiled, watching him. She could almost feel the water of Bear Lake around her—of reaching out with her hands to pull the water toward her and of kicking it behind her with her feet. She nodded happily.

"If an electric fan had enough power, it would pull itself right off the table. Wouldn't it?"

He looked at her for concurrence, then crooked his finger for her to follow. "Okay. Now let's take a look at the wing. Did you ever hold your hand out of a car window, like this, with the car going fast?" His hand was held at an inclined angle with the fingers straight. "At forty or fifty, the air really pushes your hand up. Takes some muscle power to hold it down. Now imagine your hand the size of this wing. How much do you think it would lift at fifty miles an hour?"

The shrug combined with a negative shake of the head showed how adept she had become at using gestures for communication. This he noted with sorrow.

"Almost as much as your folks' car," he told her.

She looked at the wing with new respect. Picturing her mother's Chevrolet, with this wing attached, she smiled inwardly at the idea of soaring up off the road over the other cars—of the startled expressions on the faces of observers. Then his voice invaded her thoughts.

". . . Your hand is lifted because the wind strikes the underside and is deflected downward. Remember what they told you in your physics class?" He went on before she had a chance to let him know she hadn't taken physics. "For every action there is an equal and opposite reaction. I think that came from Newton, way back in the sixteen-hundreds. You push on that tree, it pushes back at you."

She looked at the tree perplexed, unable to imagine what the tree had to do with the wind lifting her hand.

The expression on her face, a scowl and a twist of her mouth, brought forth a sudden snort of mirth from the pilot. "Okay, forget all that. Sometimes I just get carried away. What I should have said is this—if your hand is pushing the air down, then the air is pushing your hand up. That's what happens with a kite. Is that better?"

She indicated a reluctant acceptance of his explanation.

"A wing behaves a lot like a kite, but it's a little more complicated. Here, I'll show you. Go on out where you can see the end of the wing."

He waited until she was in position, then pulled down hard where the struts attached under the wing. The airplane tilted so Katie could look along the length of the wing.

"See that?" he grunted. "See how the top of the wing is curved and the bottom is flat?" After a few seconds he released his hold and the airplane rocked level.

Katie nodded.

"That shape is called an airfoil. I'm not sure I understand all about it myself, but it has something to do with the greater distance that the air has to flow over the top of the wing, as compared with what's going underneath. The air on top is stretched out . . . ," he made a motion with his hands, that suggested pulling the air apart ". . . and that makes the air thinner. Thinner air means less pressure on top of the wing, so the greater pressure on the bottom pushes the wing up. A guy named Bernoulli came up with that one."

She gave him a look that showed less than complete understanding.

He chuckled. "Don't worry about it. Not that important anyway. I'd hate to think you knew what I was talking about cause I sure don't."

She laughed aloud, thinking how much she enjoyed listening to him. In a way, he was like Bart—he did all the talking, not compelling her to speak—but in all other ways, he was different. The most notable distinction between the two was size. She stood several inches above this man. Also, he didn't have the solid appearance that Bart projected with his brown, smooth-skinned face—like polished mahogany—set on top of a massive frame.

The man before her showed a face that had not weathered well. Character lines, many and deeply eroded, were formed into a pattern that suggested a perpetual good nature. Gentle brown eyes, set back within the crevices, almost disappeared when he smiled. And he smiled often.

You noticed that the ailerons are operated by the control stick when it's moved side to side. Now keep that idea in mind and come with me."

He walked to the back of the airplane with her following. "This is the tail of the airplane. The books refer to it as the 'empennage'—French, of course. These are the elevators hinged to horizontal stabilizers." He indicated two sets of horizontal surfaces, one set extending from each side of the craft's fuselage at the extreme aft end where it tapered to a small section.

The elevators are connected to the same control stick as the ailerons and move up when you pull the stick back and down when you push the stick forward.

He enjoyed watching her make each new discovery, even more than with the others. This was better because this time it was a girl, the only one he'd ever known who'd shown any interest. And her interest was genuine. He knew that. Not feigned out of politeness or friendliness, but true absorbing interest.

He took hold and swung from side to side another yellow panel, quite similar to an elevator, but this one mounted vertically.

"The 'rudder', like you'd find on a boat. The rudder is used to steer the plane on the ground and help make turns in the air. Connects to pedals inside. Push with the right foot to turn right, left foot to turn left."

He grinned at her. Charming little elf, he thought as she turned back to the airplane. If we'd had a girl, I wonder what she would have been like. What if she'd had this girl's problems?

He rolled another cigarette and observed as she moved slowly about the cub—scrutinizing, touching. The smooth, varnished surfaces of the propeller attracted her interest. She studied, in detail, the wood-grain contours. Then she glanced at the pilot and smiled.

Finally she ducked under the wing and approached the craft's tiny enclosure. She stood for several minutes. Bent at the waist with her head and shoulders inside, her eyes roved the interior. Tentatively, she took hold of the control stick.

He saw her turn to watch the ailerons' reaction while moving the stick from side to side. Now she'll look at the elevators he guessed.

As if his thought was command, she looked back to see the elevators respond to forward and backward movements of the control stick.

Quickly she learned that the stick could be moved in a circle. The concentration showed on her face as she tried to determine how the airplane would react with each position of the control.

She remembered the rudder, then, and searched for the foot-pedals. There they are, he saw her decide. On the floor in front were a pair of tiny metal pads that were obviously intended to be foot-operated. On each side of the front seat, she saw an identical pedal. She pushed on it with her hand while watching the rudder. Nothing happened. She pushed with greater strength. The rudder remained motionless. Confused, she looked at the pilot.

He chuckled at her expression. "That's the brake pedal. The rudder bar is next to it."

She resumed her search. Adjacent to each of the small pedals, somewhat above and forward, was a much larger rectangular metal frame. The horizontal member was worn shiny. It didn't look like a pedal to Katie but, sure enough, it moved under her hand and the rudder swung on its post.

A short period of experimentation convinced the girl that the airplane would, indeed, turn right if the rudder bar on the right side were pushed. That might take some getting used to, she decided.

The little sleigh she had steered with her feet down the hills near Garden City, was exactly opposite. I had to push with my left foot to go right, she recalled. I wonder how it would feel the other way. On an impulse she started to enter the airplane, then stepped back, glancing at the pilot.

"Use the back seat," he advised. It's easier to get into."

Still she hesitated.

"It's alright. Go ahead," he urged.

I'm glad I wore slacks, she thought, clambering awkwardly into the airplane. Mother would call this, "definitely unladylike."

Once seated, she placed her feet on the rudder bars, pushing alternately left and right.

He put out the cigarette and moved alongside the open doors. "Hold the stick in your right hand and the throttle in your left. That's the throttle." He pointed to a lever with a knob on top that was positioned next to the left side window. "Now you look like a pilot."

She grinned, moved the controls and looked around.

When she leaned to the side trying to see forward, he chuckled. "Can't see much straight ahead until the tail comes up on takeoff. Then it's not too bad."

She pointed at the panel in front that held half-a-dozen gauges and asked with her eyes.

"Instruments," he announced reaching inside and pointing to each in turn as he spoke. "This one on the left and these two small ones are your engine instruments. The larger is the tachometer—shows how fast the engine and, therefore the propeller, is turning. Multiply the numbers by one-hundred. See?" She nodded.

"Swell. The other two are engine oil-temperature and oil-pressure. Along with the tach, they give you all the information you must have to know that your engine is happy."

He winked at her. "And when you're flying, you'll want to know that you've got a happy engine. I'll tell you right now, there's nothing meaner than an unhappy airplane engine.

"So much for the engine. Now these three . . ." he pointed at the instruments. ". . . show you what the airplane is doing—how fast it's going, what direction and how high. Don't believe the numbers on the airspeed indicator. This thing probably wouldn't go that fast straight down." He made a diving motion with his hand.

"The compass is just a compass. Were you a girl scout?"

She nodded.

"This one shows which direction the plane is pointed relative to north. I guess I should say 'magnetic north', which isn't the same as 'true north'. You know all about that, though. Don't you?"

Her smile was non-committal, but she was trying to remember what she had heard or read about compasses.

"Right now you're facing about . . . ," he leaned inside for a closer look. ". . . southeast, give or take a few degrees."

He waited for an affirmative nod. "Now, finally the altimeter."

She pointed upwards.

"Right. The airplane's altitude—how high. It's shown in thousands of feet above sea level. Here on the ground we're at about forty-four hundred feet, so far as I've been able to find out from the county surveyor. The altimeter can be set with this little knob."

He made a small adjustment and tapped the face of the instrument. "There. Four-thousand and, roughly, four-hundred." He turned from the instruments and looked at her. "That's our reference. Now if the airplane was flying one-thousand feet above where we are now, the altimeter would say five-thousand, four-hundred. Got that?"

She smiled.

He stepped back from under the wing, arched backwards and massaged his back. "Well that about does it. I'm happy to announce that you're a graduate from the Professor Spencer School of Aeronautics. I hereby bestow upon you the title of Aviatrix de Aeronautique Extraordinaire. I'm taking some liberties with the French, you'll notice. If you step forward you'll be awarded a diploma," he dug in his pockets, "or maybe just a book of matches."

She grinned and climbed from the airplane. With great dignity he presented the matches, standing straight and solemn. She joined in the pantomime, but the sight of his craggy face pulled into long lines caused her to collapse in a fit of giggles.

The pilot held his posture. "You do not appear to appreciate the gravity of this occasion. These ceremonies are not to be taken lightly."

She tried to collect herself, but finally turned away, bent over holding her sides.

After drying her eyes, she sneaked a look. He was standing, relaxed, grinning at her. A hiccup escaped which brought on another giggle.

Then, self-consciously, she strolled toward the back end of the airplane and he watched her idly trace, with a fingernail, the image of the little bear's face on the vertical tail surface.

Her eyes wandered around the site, taking in the mowed grass strip, the slab building, the fuel and oil drums alongside, and finally back to the man himself.

He cleared his throat. "My wife wonders the same thing."

"Huh?" Katie blurted out—confused.

He motioned toward the airplane. "What's an old fool doing playing around with kid's toys?"

Katie's eyes widened with alarm and she started making sounds of protest. "N . . . no! I . . . I . . . !"

He held up a hand, grinning. "Hey! It's okay. She's right, of course. We sure could have put the money to better use, but I guess I'm just a big kid at heart."

She felt somewhat ill at ease that he should be revealing personal matters to her. She'd never had an adult confide in her before in this manner.

The routine of making a cigarette provided an escape. He chided himself, wondering why he felt compelled to explain to this young girl. "It's those serious eyes," he decided.

"I had to convince her it was an investment—that I could make some money during the summer vacation."

Katie recognized the smell of Bull Durham tobacco as the smoke drifted past her—the same as Bart used. She waited, uncomfortably, for him to continue.

"She wanted me to work in the pea vinery again." He stood for a moment, shaking his head and staring at the ground. "God! I can't stand the smell of the place." He gave her a devilish grin. "Besides, it ain't as much fun."

She moved into the path of a wisp of smoke floating lazily in the calm air and inhaled deeply. It was an appealing aroma. For some reason. it reminded her of Garden City, the farm and her father.

"The vinery is only seven weeks work," he seemed to be talking to himself. "and the plane I can use all summer— part time in the other months."

He saw the question in her eyes. "I teach school," he answered. "No! Not a professor. I just throw around a few four-dollar words sometimes so people will think I'm smarter than I look."

They smiled together.

"I'm just a shop teacher at the junior high school. Not much else an old aviator can do. During the war, I was in the Army Air Corps—originally it was called the Air Branch of the Signal Corps. After I finished flight-training, they kept me on as an instructor so that by the time I got to France, the Armistice had been declared." He stopped to take a drag on his cigarette. "Not a single shot fired in anger. When I got back, me and a couple of buddies picked up a government surplus Jenny—a biplane trainer."

A slight frown showed on her face.

"'Biplane'. Two wings—one above the other," he gestured toward the airplane. "The Piper's a monoplane—one wing."

Katie thought the airplane had two wings—one on each side—but she shrugged with acceptance. And she didn't want to interrupt his narration.

"We got 'er for four-hundred bucks but she was almost new. I taught both those guys to fly the thing. Pretty good, too." He grinned and winked. "One of 'em has a flying operation down Ogden way. He stood for a while, smoking and staring at the mountains to the east.

Katie was becoming uneasy with the long silence but he finally turned and smiled at her, embarrassed for the lapse. "I got married and had to sell my share of the Jenny. Didn't fly for a dozen years or more. Then Uncle Henry kicked off last summer and left me some money."

She could see him losing himself in his thoughts as he talked.

"He had a dry farm up in Idaho. When I was a kid, I used to go up there during the summer and help him out. I kinda liked doing it. He talked to me like I was a grownup. Learned a lot, too."

The cigarette had burned close to his fingers. He threw it down and stepped on it. "I guess he liked me. He was an old bachelor and, except for my mother, I was his only relative. Had me in his will for a long time, they told me."

Again he grinned, squinting through the folds of skin under his eyes. She grinned back, shyly.

"Anyway, now I've got an airplane and it better be making some returns on its investment or my wife'll never let me hear the end of it. Introductory rides are three dollars." He looked at her with lifted eyebrows. "Are you ready to go?"

Chapter 10

By the offhand manner in which the question was presented, Katie failed to grasp his meaning. But when the full impact of his words registered, she gasped aloud. Her skin became hot and cold simultaneously and her legs suddenly seemed unable to provide the necessary support. The hollow feeling in the pit of her stomach made it impossible for her to draw a deep breath.

He had to laugh at the variety of expressions that showed on her face in rapid sequence—surprise, shock, fear, anticipation, apprehension.

"I . . . I . . . I . . . ," She stood before him, popeyed and trembling. trying to respond.

He decided to help her. "Do you want to?"

She hesitated, collected herself, then nodded cautiously.

"But you don't have the money with you," he guessed.

She nodded again, solemnly.

"If that's all, you can bring it next time."

Katie did some quick calculations. Two days from tomorrow she would give her mother the last of the nine dollars, then there would be another week, at least, of beet-thinning and that money would be her's to do with what she wanted. Bart was paying her a dollar a day.

"Work like a man, by God, you're gonna' get paid like a man," he had told her.

Her bright smile gave the pilot his answer.

"Let's go, then." He walked to the airplane and beckoned her to come. "In this plane the pilot sits in the back seat. Besides, you'll see better up front."

He showed her where to put her feet, where to grasp with her hands to reduce the effort of climbing into the forward seat. The odor, she had noticed earlier, was much more pronounced in front. It was a strange scent but, to the excited girl, a heady aroma. Much later she learned that the smell was primarily a combination of two ingredients: The fuel tank, located a few inches forward of Katie's knees, was prone to overflow during filling and seep raw gasoline into the aircraft's interior. Mixed with this was the essence of dope, a paint-like substance used to tighten and coat the cotton cloth that covered the structure.

"Here," he told her, "fasten this belt. It keeps the plane from falling off of you."

She was too agitated to appreciate his humor, but quickly complied.

He checked the seat belt for tightness. "Okay. Now I'm going to start the engine but I'll need some help." He waited until he had her full attention. "The starter on this machine is an 'armstrong' model—these arms," he said flexing his arm muscles. "I'll be in front of the plane, so you'll have to be the pilot and take care or things in here."

She nodded, warily.

"We'll set the throttle about so." He reached across in front of her to position the lever slightly forward. "Remember those little brake pedals?" He pointed at the cockpit floor. "Good. Put a heel on each one. That's it. Now push! Hard!"

She stiffened with the effort.

"Fine. You can relax now but if the plane starts moving, after I start the engine, you'll want to push those pedals whatever it takes to stop. By the way, the pedal on the right is for this one," he kicked the tire, "and the left pedal is for the other one." He smiled encouragement. "So far so good?"

Her return smile was somewhat strained.

"Now hold the stick all the way back. Atta' girl." He studied her for a moment, noting the determination in the set of her jaw. Gutsy lil' cuss, he thought.

"One more thing—see the switch up over your left shoulder? It's got positions for off, left, right and both."

She found the switch above the side window.

"That's for the engine ignition. When I say 'contact', turn the switch to 'both'. Then stand on the brakes, pull the stick back and put your hand on the throttle. Got that?"

She mentally reviewed the sequence, going through the motions. Finally she looked at him with wide eyes.

"You'll be alright," he chuckled. "Just remember, if the plane starts to move, even though you're applying brakes, pull the throttle all the way back. If that doesn't stop it, turn the switch off." He patted her shoulder for assurance and started forward.

A thought occurred to him and he turned back. "This thing makes more noise than a car so don't let that scare you. It's perfectly normal."

Like Bart's tractor, she remembered.

Sitting high in the seat to see past the engine cowl, she watched as he moved in front of the airplane. He took hold of one blade of the propeller and flung it downward while, as part of the same quick motion, stepped back out of the way. The propeller turned once and jiggled to a stop. This was repeated several times. Then he looked at the girl behind the windshield and yelled, "brakes and contact."

He saw her reach for the switch, make the setting and turn to look forward. Her expression told him that the brakes were being applied with true dedication. One more jerk on the propeller and it disappeared in a blur as the engine clattered to life. His casual stroll around the wing strut to the door seemed to Katie nothing short of out-and-out dallying.

With an ease born of practice he slipped into the back seat, fastened his safety belt and closed the two-piece door. "I've got it," he told her. "Sit back and enjoy the ride."

With a gasp of relief, the girl released the controls and collapsed back into her seat.

The engine tempo increased and the airplane began to move, wings rocking as the doughnut tires rolled on the rough turf.

It does sound like Bart's tractor, Katie decided.

"No. I'm not drunk," he called out. "I have to zigzag to see where I'm going."

This was obvious to Katie, who was peering from side to side as the airplane weaved its way to the end of the field. Looking down next to her seat, she watched the pilot's boots on the rudder bars and correlated their movements with the turns.

After he steered the airplane near the field boundary fence, the bouncing stopped and the engine idled. "I'm going to check the magnetos now," she heard him say. "This engine uses two for its ignition so there's always one working in case the other goes bad."

She had turned in her seat to watch.

"Set the switch on 'L' and only the magneto on the left side is used. 'R' is for the right mag. We normally operate with both for maximum power."

He put his hand on the throttle. "I'm going to set the engine for about nineteen-hundred rpm. You can see it on the tachometer." He pointed to the instrument in front of her. "Then I'll switch one mag off at a time to see how much the engine slows down. Ready?"

Katie saw the needle on the instrument move and settle on the mark representing the number nineteen as the engine roared. She heard a slight change in the beat and the needle wavered slightly below the mark. This happened twice. Then he reached past her left arm and pulled a black knob that was set in a small, recessed panel under the side window. Again the engine tempo changed with the tachometer registering a noticeable reduction.

"That's the carburetor heat control," he told her after returning the knob to its original position and throttling the engine to idle. "It puts hot air into the carburetor if it's wet and cold enough for ice to be forming. That check was to make sure it works. Now, one more thing . . . ," he made several turns on a little crank under the left side window next to Katie's seat—it looked like a window crank in her mother's car, ". . . set the trim and we're in business. I'll show you later what it does."

He peered around her at the instrument panel. "Everything else looks okay."

The control stick in front of Katie moved in a circle bumping her leg. "Sorry," he said. "You'll have to keep away from the controls."

Jerking her legs apart, she told herself, yes mother—definitely unladylike!

This thought and all others vanished as the engine sound increased and the airplane moved again.

"We use full power for takeoff," he yelled as he steered the craft into alignment with the grass strip.

Katie was unprepared for the clamor produced by the machine as the throttle was pushed forward to its limit. The bumps quickly became a series of bounces with the increasing speed. As the tail lifted, a breathless passenger was presented with a view down the length of the field and the fence across the end that was approaching at an alarming rate.

Then the bouncing stopped. She felt herself lifted, saw the road appear off to the left beyond the trees and glimpsed the fence as it flashed beneath. After that, the wonder of the moment took over and fear was gone.

A panorama of color and form opened around her. Oh my God, she thought. I can't believe this. Look at the fields—they're like different colored cloth patches, sewed together to make a quilt.

The fields were outlined by the darker greens of weeds, bushes and trees growing along fences and ditches. She looked down and saw livestock in the fields shrinking before her eyes.

A farm came into view next to the road—the house, barn and outbuildings miniaturized on a carpet of browns and greens.

It's just like that model village they had displayed in the ZCMI store when I was a little girl, she thought.

Magically, she was the child again, several hundred feet tall. Looking at the toy farm, she could see horses in corrals with feed-stalls and troughs all made with exquisite attention to detail. A row of trees was set in front of the house and a garden alongside. In back was the clothesline. Even a toy automobile had been placed in the yard.

A shoe box and a Mother's Oats box had been cleverly fashioned and painted to resemble a barn and silo. She could almost make out the image of the rooster on the weather vane.

But then Katie caught sight of a woman walking at the side of the road pushing a baby-carriage and the spell was broken. Further along she saw two boys on a horse herding a small cluster of cows. They waved at the airplane and Katie, laughing, waved back.

Now it's me up here, she thought, waving at someone else on the ground.

Bear River passed underneath, its winding path across the valley floor marked by wild growth of brush and trees. The river half circled the dismantled Amalgamated Sugar Company factory. Here the remnants stood, a big warehouse and a towering smokestack, conspicuous in their setting among the quiet little farms. The airplane turned so that, for an instant, Katie could look directly down into the black opening of the chimney.

She turned and grinned at the pilot. The grin faded abruptly, however, when the pilot pulled back on the throttle control so that the engine roar subsided, leaving only the whistling sounds of air rushing past outside.

"Where do you live in Smithfield?" he asked the wide-eyed girl.

"Huh?" Most of her attention was given to the quieted engine.

"We're not going to fall," he assured her. "What part of town?"

She managed, with some effort, to focus on his question and stammer an answer, "S . . . s . . . south."

Nodding, he restored power and smiled at the obvious relief this brought to his passenger.

Katie's interest intensified as familiar features of the terrain appeared below.

Everything looks so different from up here, she thought, but now I know where we are. He's following the road between Amalga and Smithfield. I recognize those two houses on the north side.

Those were the only structures between town and the small, separated farms that were collectively known as Amalga. Then they passed over the railroad yard at the edge of the community and were soon cruising above First North Street toward Main Street.

The tabernacle and Summit grade school were clustered around a tiny park that appeared on the right side.

The girl sat straight and tall in her seat looking out one side window and then the other. Like a queen on a throne. The pilot wondered what thoughts were running through her mind.

A gradual, sweeping turn brought the flight of the airplane on the east side and parallel with Main Street, which was also the highway that scribed a straight line through the center of town—continuing to the ends of the valley and beyond. The Bamburger trolley station passed under the right wing. Katie began looking for her house as they approached the Del Monte cannery on the south side of town. She spotted Bart's big barn first and yelled with excitement—pointing.

Then she saw the house. How wretched it appeared from her elevated perch—faded yellow, boxy little dwelling with hardly any yard. One small tree and the old Chevrolet stood in front. With mixed emotions, Katie scanned the place that was, at different times, her shelter, confinement, sanctuary, heaven and hell. She searched carefully for her secret place in the pasture and smiled when it was located.

At that moment she caught sight of her mother, standing at the backdoor of the house, watching the circling airplane. Terrified, she shrank away from the window.

If she knew it was me up here . . . . She didn't dare finish the thought. Instead she pretended intense interest in something out the other side window and the pilot obediently turned in that direction.

Smithfield was left behind and Katie relaxed but only momentarily. The engine slowed and she heard the pilot ask, "Want to fly it?"

She jerked her head around to see if he was serious.

"It's easy. Take hold of the stick—I'll show you."

Still she hesitated.

"Go ahead. It won't bite." His smile was reassuring.

Tentatively she put her hand on the control.

Just a couple of things to remember—push forward you go down, pull back you go up, left and right as you need to keep the wings level." He moved the stick to demonstrate as he spoke. "Look over the nose at the horizon. You should try to hold the front end of the airplane about there to stay at this altitude."

He gradually applied throttle and the craft began climbing. Katie sat frozen, not daring to move the stick. With a touch on the shoulder he got her attention and signaled for forward motion.

Cautiously she complied and was rewarded with a much larger view of the Cache Valley countryside rising in the windshield.

He reduced engine power to be heard more easily. "Not quite that much, Katie. Pull back a little."

As the airplane leveled under her urging, he continued with a gentle patter. "Atta' girl! You're doing fine. Now hold it about there. That's right, you won't harm anything. Make the airplane do what you want it to do—you're the one in charge."

The engine roar returned and Katie settled herself to gain mastery over this machine. After all, she had driven Bart's tractor and the cars, hadn't she? And Bart had told her about the same thing: "Drive the goddamn thing, Katie, don't let it drive you."

A few experimental oscillations and the southern hills settled into a fixed position on the windshield. She soon learned that very slight changes in pressure on the stick were all that was needed to alter the craft's attitude.

The altimeter caught her attention. The needle was near the number six.

I'll try to stay at six-thousand feet, she told herself.

A few minutes later she noted an increase on the instrument so she countered with slight forward pressure on the control.

She felt a tap on her shoulder and looked back. The pilot was holding both hands up and indicating, with a nod, for her to do likewise. She frowned at this suggestion but, reluctantly, released the stick. The airplane tilted upward, as expected. Her raised eyebrows said, now what?

He pointed to the small crank next to her left arm. Under his direction, she began clockwise rotation of the crank, glancing suspiciously at the side window. The window remained closed but the aircraft tilted forward and began descending. She reversed the rotation and was obliged to see the gentle climb restored. After a period of trial and error. she determined the position that maintained a constant altitude with the need to apply pressure on the control stick only occasionally when the delicate balance was upset. Holding up both hands, she turned and smiled her victory at the pilot.

Logan city had slipped slowly past on the left before he directed her to make a turn to the right. Her face was set in a mask of concentration as she pondered the maneuver. Finally she applied side pressure to the control stick. The long wing canted and the airplane began a sweeping turn.

When she glanced back at the pilot, he was hunched up against the side of the enclosure away from the turn and staring, with feigned horror, at the wing pointing toward the ground. Then he grinned and she realized he was mocking the position she had taken when the turn began. He took hold of her shoulders and firmly centered her back on the seat. The look he received in return was one of pretended annoyance and he laughed aloud.

At his signal, she straightened the airplane so they were retracing their path of flight up the valley. Then, cautiously at first, she began making turns, left and right, remembering not to lean away from the turn. She smiled to herself, wondering if someone on the ground was watching the meandering airplane. She hoped so.

Once more the engine's roar diminished until there was only the sound of air sweeping past the fuselage. "We're landing a few miles ahead," he answered her quizzical look, "so we've got to start going down. I've got some students that will be showing up pretty soon."

The disappointment was obvious on her face.

"Keep on flying," he said quickly, "but in that direction," he pointed, "and hold it at sixty miles per hour."

She looked at the instrument marked "Air Speed" and saw that it registered near seventy.

"Pull back on the stick to slow down and use the trim crank to hold it."

Soon she had the airplane gliding at near the prescribed speed.

The pilot smiled with satisfaction. He'd been right about her—she was bright and quick. "Do you see Loganna?" he asked. "That's it sitting out there all alone. Fly over the top of it."

She watched the building, that housed the public swimming pool, until it disappeared under the front-end of the airplane.

"Put your feet on the rudder bars—but not the brakes—so you can feel what I'm doing to make a landing. Keep hold of the stick."

She felt the controls move under her hands and feet. The engine roared briefly, then was still again. Scanning the fields ahead, she finally saw the strip and the little building next to the road.

"Use the rudder to stay lined-up with the strip," he spoke while moving the controls for emphasis. "Use the stick to keep the wings level and hold your speed. Use the throttle if you're too low."

Katie watched the approaching grass field, trying to sense what the pilot was doing. Another blast of sound from the engine and they were floating over the fence that marked the near boundary of the field. "Hold 'er off until she's ready to quit flying," she heard.

At this point the craft's wheels were skimming the grass—the engine cowling rising in front of the windshield until it blocked all vision ahead. Then the first touch of a wheel came, a slight bounce and the fat little tires were rolling on the uneven surface.

After the airplane had tottered back to its berth, Katie sat in a daze, overwhelmed by events of the day.

"Better take it off." She came out of her trance to realize he was standing beside the airplane grinning at her. "You'd look pretty silly wearing it around."

It took a moment before she grasped his meaning. Then she laughed and unfastened the safety belt.

After she had extricated herself from the airplane, after an embarrassing period when she had tried to express her appreciation, still she lingered—reluctant to end the enchantment. Stroking the smooth fabric, she decided, I'll call you Mister Piper.

She remembered almost nothing of the long bike ride home.

Chapter 11

She couldn't imagine what had come over her daughter. An absolute little bitch before last week, Clara recalled. Something had happened. Her mother's instincts told her that.

"I can't for the life of me understand why you want to keep doing that filthy work now that you've paid for the glasses. That water is practically mud."

Katie lifted one leg out of the bath water and applied soap liberally. "He asked m . . . m . . . me." She carefully avoided looking at her mother.

The older woman frowned—she knew the signs. "Surely there's enough boys around this town. He ought to be able to find someone."

Her daughter lowered her leg into the tub and shrugged.

Clara released a sigh of exasperation. "Well hurry up and get out of there. Supper's getting cold."

I guess I should be glad, the perplexed mother told herself. Her disposition has certainly improved.

She walked into the kitchen and stood at the window looking out over the pasture.

Going back over events of the past several days, she tried to find a clue to her daughter's behavior. Like a bear with a sore paw until last week.

She thought of Katie returning home from the beet field, dirty, drawn with fatigue, almost too tired to bathe or eat and sullenly handing over the dollar she had been paid. Clara's heart had ached looking at her. On several occasions she had weakened in her resolve to carry through with the girl's discipline even though she knew it had to be done.

The first day had been most difficult. She had found her woman-child that evening in exhausted sleep. Still in her work clothes, she was lying on top of the bed cover—the lines in her young face softened, her sunburnt lips slightly parted. The mother had stood at the foot of the bed and wept.

So unhappy, my poor darling, she had agonized. It should be the most enjoyable period of your life instead of living with this misery. Tears of helplessness and frustration, had flowed, unheeded by the sleeping girl.

Why her? Clara had said to herself again. Why this damn stuttering? One little flaw and her whole life is being ruined. If it was the croup or a broken arm or even appendicitis, something could be done. But this! The mother had raged. What can I do?

She had cried for her daughter's plight and for herself. Her husband should have been at her side providing the comfort and reassurance that she was doing the right thing.

The bewildered mother stood at the window, pondering. She never could lie worth a damn. She doesn't look at me when she's lying. Clara shook her head. But why lie? It must be a boy!

She tried to recall their conversation of the previous Sunday afternoon when the girl had returned.

"R . . . r . . . rid . . . in' my b . . . b . . . b . . . bike," Katie had answered the inquiry—the stammer worse.

"Where, for heaven's sake?"

"B . . . Ben . . . Ben . . . sss . . . son W . . . Ward, and A . . . A . . . Amal . . . ga." She had made a vague waving motion in the general direction of those two communities, keeping her eyes averted.

"For five hours?" Clara had marveled at the resiliency of youth. "If I'd put in a week like that, I would have spent all day in bed."

Katie had shrugged.

"I can't, for the life of me, understand what's so interesting about Benson Ward or Amalga," she had persisted. "Who do you know there?"

"Beth. K . . . K . . . Kathy."

Clara had remembered the two girls had been classmates of her daughter in junior high school.

"Since when were you that friendly with Beth and Kathy," she said. "I can't imagine why you'd want to ride that far to see them."

Finally she had dropped the subject but as Katie's high spirits became obvious, her suspicions intensified. It's got to be a boy!

Still drying her close-cropped hair as she entered the kitchen, the girl was actually humming even though her fatigue showed in the way she moved.

Clara looked at her, concerned. "When will you finish Bart's beets?"

"Next w. . .week," came the answer.

"Then you'll be done?"

Katie shook her head. "I'll hoe h . . . h . . . his c . . . c . . . corn." Seeing her mother's frown, she went on quickly, "N . . . not so h . . . h . . . hard. P . . . pay's the same."

The mother stared steadily at her daughter for a long period while the young girl tried to hold an appearance of nonchalance.

"It's your life," Clara said at last.

* * *

She kept the books with her lunch at the end of the field. There they waited for her—a goal, a reward—tantalizing with their treasures. Fifteen minutes she allowed herself after each circuit of the field, after four rows of the spindly plants—rows that appeared to be without end—had been reduced to a single plant every ten to twelve inches. But it was so much easier when she could spend the time going over in her mind passages from the books.

After a drink, she would sit on the ditch-bank, knees up, heels digging into the dirt and read from Amelia Earhart's "The Fun Of It". She had read the book in its entirety but then she returned, again and again to the chapter titled "When You Learn To Fly". It seemed to Katie that the great aviatrix was talking directly to her. Everything was

described in a manner that made it easy for her to compre-
hend. Women can tell it so much better, Katie decided.
Smug in her new-found knowledge, she read with delight the
use of the "stick" and the "rudder bar" to control the airplane
and concluded that she had done better on her first attempt
than Miss Earhart.

The author's treatise of "stunt-flying"— slips, stalls
and spins, the "three S's", as given in the book—provoked a
sense of uncertainty in her young reader. Katie recalled her
one experience riding the "Devil's Loop" during the
Smithfield Mayday carnival. If asked, she would never have
been able to explain what compelled her to do so against the
advice of her mother and Maggie Sorenson. Maggie had
kept repeating, "You're gonna get sick."

After several circuits, the world had commenced to
spin in a blur past her staring eyes. Shortly afterward, she
had realized the wisdom of Maggie's warning, for it had
occurred, quite suddenly and at a most inopportune moment.
With her tightly strapped body sitting inverted, she'd been
subjected to a shower of her own vomit.

I don't think I'd be able to do any "stunting", she decided, using Amelia's word. Not that it matters. It's so
expensive I can't afford to fly very much.

Nevertheless, she was comforted by Miss Earhart's
assurance that most people don't suffer "air sickness" after
the first exposure. There had been no "bumps in the air"
during her two flights with Mister Spencer so Katie wondered how well she might fare under worse conditions. She
had been in a boat on Bear Lake and been rocked by the
waves. She thought it was exciting, but that was a long time
ago. Maybe she didn't have the "strong stomach" Amelia
implied was essential for dealing with "waves in the air".
Her laugh had a hollow ring when she read Miss Earhart's
statement concerning the fatalistic attitude of certain
passengers:

". . . of course, some people seem almost determined
to be ill. I have heard them say to airline attendants before
they get in:

'Well, I'm going to be a very bad passenger today.'

'Why do you think so?' asks the transport employee.

'I know I shall be sick.' And by concentrating thus on the idea, some do manage very nicely!"

* * *

Mister Spencer had somewhat allayed her fears with his explanation of turbulence.

"Air is a lot like water. Water sits still at lower temperatures but if you set a pan full on a stove and heat it up so it starts boiling, it churns and rolls around. That's because the water, at the bottom of the pan where it's hottest, changes into vapor which expands and rises. Air behaves much the same. When it's heated from the ground, it expands and rises. It also churns and rolls around just like the boiling water.

"You also get turbulence when air is being blown across the land. It goes up and down and around hills the way the Logan river flows over and around those big boulders up in the canyon. A plane gets bounced around in that turbulent air just like a boat in rough water.

"When you fly out of an area where the air is moving in one direction into an adjacent area where the air is moving in another direction, you feel the change as a bump.

"Airplanes are designed strong enough to withstand turbulence. Otherwise there'd be planes falling out of the sky all over the place. The ride in rough air may not be the most comfortable, but it's safe unless you're going like a bat out of hell. The trick is to slow down when it gets really choppy. You'd do that in a boat.

"Now remember, I'm talking about flying in good weather. You're almost always going to get some turbulence when there's clouds around. But then you wouldn't think of going out to poke holes in clouds, would you? Let me tell you something else—there's clouds and then there's clouds! Those little cotton balls that you can see hanging over the mountains, they wouldn't bother you much. You'd get a little shake if you plowed through them but nothing to worry about.

"It's the thunderheads you've got to watch out for—you know, the ones that are black underneath and go up halfway to heaven. I don't speak from personal experience, but they say that inside those you'll find vertical winds of more than a hundred miles per hour and hail as big as baseballs. You fly that little Cub into a thunderhead, you'll have those yellow wings wrapped around your ears and only a short time to make peace with your maker.

"I've flown in air so wild I was sure I'd be wearing my belt as a collar, but the wings have always stayed hooked on. Of course I've never been inside a thunderhead or I probably wouldn't be here now."

Regardless of what Mister Spencer said, Katie knew that she would prefer not having those "waves in the air" when she flew.

It was the author's description of the view from above that held Katie's interest most intensely—almost as if Amelia had been in the Piper Cub with her. Reading from the book, she could visualize Cache Valley: the fields, the mountains, the woods, the river, the farms and the towns.

Amelia knew exactly what it was like, Katie realized. I hope Miss Earhart is still alive so that someday I can write a letter and let her know how much I liked her book.

Missus Albright at the library had told her about the disappearance of the famous woman flyer while trying to fly around the world. Katie couldn't remember hearing about the occurrence when it happened. Such things didn't interest her at the time. Now she felt as if she may have lost a close friend.

The other book, "Everyman's Book Of Flying" by Orville Hayter Kneen, she read doggedly trying to gain a better understanding of the "aeronautics" that had been described by Mister Spencer—she could not yet think of him as "Crow". That's such a terrible name to call a man, she thought.

The chapter dealing with "Principles Of Flight" caused her head to spin with its references to: "inclined planes", "boundary layer", "thrust", "air density", "angle of attack", "camber" and "vacuum lift". Mister Spencer's explanations of "lift" were a lot easier to understand than those in the book, but after reading a few paragraphs and thinking about it through four rows of beets, it began to make sense.

She had checked the two books out of the library on the afternoon following "that day". Already she had established that day as the pivotal point in her life. Things that had happened to her before, were distinctly separated from everything else that had occurred since, by that day. Never in her young life, so far as she was able to recall, had she ever experienced a day that could possibly compare with that day. Never had she been so excited, frightened, thrilled and fulfilled all at the same time. In her mind she went over every detail again and again, enjoying the shivering stimulation that her thoughts provoked.

Two weeks ago, when the yellow airplane came again she had followed its flight path around the valley, shading her eyes with her hand to keep it in sight until she saw it descend near Benson Ward. At that moment, she'd made up her mind she was going to search out and find its roost. This objective became an all-consuming obsession and she began immediately making plans: when, how, what to take, how to dress and (most importantly) what to tell her mother. No thought was given to any aspect of this adventure beyond seeing the airplane up close and perhaps the man who had waved to her. For some reason, she would have never been able to explain, she wanted to see the space he had occupied, look through the windows and try to imagine what he had seen of the girl in the pasture.

That following Sunday morning she dressed carefully, putting on a clean blouse and slacks.

"You're not going to church like that!" her mother said.

"Going r . . . r . . . riding," she answered.

"Wouldn't hurt you to go to church once in a while."

Katie showed sour face—a distasteful expression. She hated church. Old Missus Smith was always trying to get her to talk about the lessons in class. Why does the church have classes, anyway? she wondered. Just like school!

"When will you be back?" her mother persisted.

Her answer was a noncommittal shrug that brought out an frustrated sigh from the older woman.

After she had finished her bowl of oatmeal, Katie put a thick slice of bread and an apple in a bag and dashed out the door.

It was the farthest she had ever ridden her bicycle. For a while she relished the exercise, feeling the cool morning air on her arms and face as her strong young muscles answered the demands of the task. The farm roads that zigzagged between fields provided her a sense of adventure that comes with seeing unfamiliar places. On two occasions she made the wrong choice of direction where the road divided and was forced to retrace her route.

By the time she intersected the Benson Ward road, her legs had tired so that pedaling became difficult. And later, seeing the Logan temple on the hill only a few miles ahead, she was about ready to give up. Then she sighted the airplane.

Thinking about it, that first glimpse of the bright yellow craft sitting on the green grass in the morning sun, she felt again the delicious tingle she had experienced at that moment. It was a picture painted in her memory that never faded. She could call up the image at will because it was at that exact instant of time that her life changed.

Katie was sure she would remember everything that happened on that day forever. And now with last Sunday, she had the memories of two exciting days to dwell upon, for last Sunday had been special also.

She had found the pilot sitting in the sun in front of the little hangar—the cub was still inside. He didn't seem surprised seeing her and merely nodded when she gave him the three dollars.

"I charge six dollars an hour for flying instruction," he told her directly. "After you solo—'solo' is when you fly by yourself—then you pay only five for the use of the airplane. First lessons are thirty to forty minutes until you learn to relax. Then we can stretch 'em a little."

He smiled at her then—a smile that made his face look like a jolly prune. "Do you want to start today?"

Katie hesitated for a brief moment. She couldn't truthfully have said that she wasn't looking forward to the possibility of flying again—otherwise, why had she brought the rest of her money? But all that remained from her week's work, after paying her mother the rest of the nine dollars and Mister Spencer three dollars, was one dollar. She wondered if that would buy ten minutes of flying.

"Little short?" He read the expression on her face correctly. "I expect you're good for it. Pay me next time."

Her smile of relief dimmed suddenly when he asked her age.

"S ... S ... seven ... t ... teen," she answered, nervously wondering if she should have said "eighteen" or even "twenty-one".

"And is this okay with your folks?"

Her quick nod showed she had anticipated the question.

"Fine," he said. "This time you take the back seat."

Chapter 12

A routine had developed. Six days a week of hoeing corn, beans and potatoes, belonged to Bart, but the seventh was her's for flying, sometimes with both morning and afternoon lessons.

Katie's hands had grown callused and hard. Long, sinewy, brown arms extended from the short or rolled up sleeves of assorted cast off blouses, generally tied in front of her scant midriff. The patched pants she wore, held up by the good graces of a sturdy belt, were consistently baggy and deficient in length by several inches.

She had yielded to her mother's insistence and bought a wide-brimmed straw-hat and work gloves—cost almost seventy cents—but these were usually found laying on the ditch bank at the end of the field, as were her shoes. The bottom of her feet had toughened against the rock-like clods of dirt so that she wore the raggedy oxfords only when leaving the house and for coming home where her mother's disapproval of bare feet would, otherwise, be waiting.

Bart continued paying her one dollar a day. The money, however, was barely covering Katie's flying expenses in spite of the fact that she was becoming unscrupulously frugal. This proved to be another source of consternation to Clara. She had never thought her daughter stingy. Of course she's never earned much money before, the mother reminded herself.

If asked what she was doing with her money, Katie would shrug or squirm uncomfortably. She had caught up with her back payments and had since made it a policy to give Crow the money she had remaining in advance—usually the full six dollars—so that he could adjust the instruction period accordingly. She shrewdly guessed that he would add a little extra time to her lesson without charge. Two thirty minute lessons on Sunday often added up to an hour and half. He laughed at himself for being such a soft touch. Sure got me figured, the little con-artist.

As the summer weeks slipped away, she progressed through: coordinated turns, climbing and descending turns, crosswind "S" turns across a reference line on the ground (usually a road), landings, takeoffs, slow-flight and eventually the "three S's"—slips, stalls and spins—she had read about in Amelia Earhart's book.

Slips weren't so bad. These were normally used in flying the Piper Cub and similar airplanes that were not equipped with "flaps". Katie had learned from Crow, and her reading, that flaps were used to slow the craft by "increasing its drag", as stated in the books she read. Hinged to the aft edge of each wing, inboard of the ailerons, these panels functioned by deflecting downward in unison to act as air brakes. Slips performed the same function, as Katie had gleaned from her training. Lowering a wing by sideways displacement of the control stick and applying opposite rudder to prevent turning, caused the airplane to fly out of alignment with its flight path, thus presenting the broad side of the craft's fuselage to the slipstream.

Katie was gratified to learn that she had the "strong stomach" that Amelia Earhart had made reference to in her book. She wasn't quite so concerned anymore with the "bumps in the air", although she preferred it smooth. Even the stall and spin training she had survived with no great discomfort.

"It's the concentration," Crow had told her. "When all your attention is on flying, you forget about your stomach."

Even so, she had little enthusiasm for Amelia's "stunt flying" and was relieved when the stall and spin instruction was finished.

Crow had made it a point to explain each planned exercise before the flight was begun. "More efficient way to learn," he'd told her during her first lesson. "Here on the ground, where it's nice and quiet, I'll describe the things we'll be working on. Then we'll go flying. Afterwards we'll talk about it. You'll have it coming at you three ways."

He had talked at great length about stalls and spins. "Stall and spin training are extremely important. If you ever get hurt in an airplane, it will most likely happen with the airplane stalled and possibly spinning under the wrong conditions."

Her look of concern had brought a smile to the crinkled face of her instructor.

"I'm going to teach you these maneuvers under the right conditions and it'll be perfectly safe. If it wasn't safe, I wouldn't even get in that airplane. I'm too much of a coward to be doing anything dangerous."

She thought about asking why he had enlisted to fight in the Air Corps if he was such a coward. She didn't, of course.

"We learn about stalls and spins for only one reason," he'd told her. "To avoid getting into those situations unintentionally.

"Stalls occur when the airplane is moving too slowly through the air to be supported by the wings. Then it drops like a rock. If you're close to the ground and ready to land, it's okay. Under these conditions, you stall the plane intentionally to make a 'three-point landing'—that's when the three wheels touchdown at the same time the wing quits lifting.

"The only other time you do intentional stalls is when you're more than two-thousand feet above the ground. Then you're doing it for practice—to get the feel of the airplane so you recognize when a stall is about to take place. That way you learn how to prevent a stall and how to recover normal flight after the stall.

"Now the airplane will tell you when it's close to a stall. The air flowing over the wing starts to swirl around— like water behind a rock in a fast running river. The elevator gets buffeted by this turbulent air and it shakes the control stick. At this point, if you increase the airspeed by applying more engine power, or by pushing forward on the control stick—or both—you'll stop the stall. But if you continue to lose airspeed, you'll get a full stall and you'll know it. The front end of the airplane will pitch down and you'll be looking at mother earth coming toward you through the windshield. Your stomach will feel the same as it does when you're in a car going fast over that big bump on the Benson Ward road where the road goes over the canal. You know the one I mean, don't you?

"Anyway, with the airplane diving at the ground you'll soon pick up enough airspeed for the wing to provide lift. Then you'll be flying again so you can pull out of the dive. You'll have lost quite a bit of altitude, however, so you'll be glad you started high. Otherwise you wouldn't be getting home for supper.

"Now normally that ol' Cub stalls at about forty miles per hour carrying two people. At that speed—and here we're talking 'airspeed', which is a lot faster than 'ground speed' at this altitude—the lift capability of the wing is equal to the weight of the airplane plus the load: gas, people, baggage and your lucky rabbit's foot. With just one person, the stalling speed is going to be about thirty-five miles per hour since the load isn't as great.

"But that plane can be made to stall at sixty or more under certain conditions. For example, if you could get that thing off the ground with a thousand-pound load—which you wouldn't be able to do at this elevation—the stalling speed would be much higher.

"There's another way it can happen, however, that has killed or hurt a lot of inexperienced pilots. Suppose you want to show off your new piloting skills to your folks. You take off and fly out to the house. There you get to circling and watching to see if someone comes outside for a look at your marvelous demonstration of aeronautics. But you forget to attend to your flying. Your angle of bank—you know, wing tilt—increases without your knowing because you're looking at the ground. To hold your altitude you compensate by pulling harder on the stick.

"At this point, centrifugal force is playing a big hand. You remember that stuff about centrifugal force and mass-inertia, don't you? An object in motion wants to continue at the same velocity in a straight line unless some force is acting on it—more Sir Isaac Newton. Your airplane wants to fly straight but the air pressure on the wing is applying the force that's holding it in the turn. Now, assuming your speed is staying about the same, the force needed to hold the plane in the turn becomes greater as the circle gets smaller. You can find out all about this by tying something on the end of a string and whirling it around your head. The faster it's whirled, the more it pulls on the string.

"Since the same forces are acting on your body, you feel yourself getting heavier as the turn gets tighter. Your butt is being pushed down into the seat and that's where you should feel it first—in your butt." He slapped his buttocks. "Your butt will be telling you that you're loading up the airplane—the airplane is getting heavier due to centrifugal force. Okay, what does it take to hold up a heavier airplane? Either a bigger wing or more airspeed, right? Your wing isn't going to grow any bigger and if your airspeed doesn't increase, you're in for what is called a 'high-speed stall'. That plane will probably flip upside down and if you don't have enough altitude to recover, you're going to make a big hole in the ground.

"So think about that whenever you're flying in a circle. Keep the circle nice and wide. And listen to your butt!

"While we're on the subject of stalls, I'd better say a few words about spins, also, since the two are related. Spins usually result from doing something out of the ordinary with the controls while the airplane is in a stall. The way we make that Cub spin is to stall it with the stick all the way back and then give it full rudder—doesn't matter which way. That ol' Cub will drop its nose and start going down, spinning like a maple leaf."

His remark had reminded Katie of the maple tree that had stood over her secret place in Bart's pasture.

"So now we've got this airplane heading for the ground like a whirling dervish. A stall got it started and it's still stalled. What do you need to get out of a stall?"

Katie shrugged.

"Airspeed! You've got to get that wing working again.

"It wasn't understood, for a long time, that a spinning airplane is really in a full stall. A lot of pilots got killed not knowing this. When they got into a spin with the nose of the airplane pointing down, their instinct was to pull back on the stick to level out. Worse thing they could have done. This just kept the plane stalled. Finally some guy must have figured 'what the hell have I got to lose' so he took his feet off the rudder bar and pushed the stick forward. This got his airspeed back and he flew out of the spin. He lived to tell about it and a bunch of pilot's lives were saved. Maybe even mine and yours.

"So that's the lesson. If you're in a stall or spin, push forward on the stick to recover—don't pull back. The spin will stop quicker if you 'kick opposite rudder'. That's pilot talk for pushing the rudder bar that's not the one you used to start the spin in the first place.

"Alright, let's go flying."

Katie had been terrified during her first spin experience. After learning that she had full control over the situation, her fears had subsided to some degree. Even though she mastered stalls and spins, it was without enjoyment.

Nor had she cared for loops.

One day Crow had demonstrated this maneuver of flying a vertical circle. "You don't need to know how to perform a loop to get a flying license," he'd said, "but someday you may get the urge to try one. When you do, I want you to do it right. A lot of pilots stall out of a loop because they don't have enough speed to start with and because they apply too much back-pressure on the stick at the top of the loop and stall the airplane. Here, I'll show you. See if you can tell how many loops we make."

Katie had counted the world going past the wind-shield three times. It had almost been three times too many with the memory still lingering of the "Devil's Loop" at the Mayday carnival.

That was all behind her now. She thought it had been going well. This morning he'd suggested that they work on takeoffs and landings for a while before leaving the pattern to go out and do air work. She had finally become comfort-able with maintaining directional control on the ground, although this had come recently. It had been difficult breaking the natural reflex habit she'd acquired as a child riding her sled down the crusted snow slopes west of Garden City. Pushing the steering bar with the left foot had caused the runners to flex and turn the sled to the right—opposite the direction the airplane turned. The final solution had come when Crow had her pump right and left pedals alternately, in rapid succession, while the airplane rolled tail high along the grassy strip. In this manner she'd learned to compensate by pushing the correct pedal with greater force or holding the pedal depressed somewhat longer in order to steer the craft as desired. Eventually her feet had become conditioned to produce the necessary response without the special technique.

In addition, she could now think with "two heads"—the expression Crow used to describe holding the airplane directionally aligned with the pedals while keeping the wings level with side movements of the control stick.

"Like rubbing your stomach with one hand while pat-ting your head with the other," he'd told her.

Learning to make acceptable landings had been the most difficult part of the training and had required the most practice. Third and fourth dimensions of control became most crucial during landings. Proper pressure on the stick, forward or backward, was needed to maintain glide speed. Wings were held level, simultaneously, by left or right sideward force applied to the stick. Meanwhile the foot-operated rudder bars were used to keep the craft directionally aligned and the height was controlled by the appropriate application of throttle.

"There isn't time to analyze which particular control is required and then execute it," the instructor had told her. "You have to feel it and respond automatically. Practice is the only way to acquire this 'feel'.

"In the final phase of landing—in that moment when it becomes necessary to stop the aircraft's descent and hold it barely off the ground until velocity decreases and the wing can no longer support the weight—the demands made on the pilot's judgment and reflexes are most critical," he'd told her.

But now it had all started to come together. That last landing had been extra good, she judged as she weaved a serpentine path through the grass toward the south end of the strip in preparation for another takeoff.

"Hold it right here," he told her unfastening his safety belt.

Braking to a stop, she frowned with curiosity as he opened the upper and lower sections of the door and climbed out. As he nonchalantly refastened the belt over the seat-cushion—not looking at her—curiosity became perplexity.

"Think I'll have a smoke," he told her with ornate calmness. "Make three landings and pick me up."

Realization was like a slap in the face. She suddenly felt unable to draw a deep breath. Her mouth opened but no sound came.

He stood for a moment with the breeze from the propeller whipping his hair and shirt. "Remember, it's going to climb faster and glide farther without me in there."

With that, he closed the door and window. As he turned and walked away, she was seized with a loneliness like she'd never known before and at the same time an overwhelming anticipation. Looking forward she saw the whole windshield and the whole instrument panel.

Can this be me? she asked herself. Am I really doing this? She looked at her hand holding the control stick. The feel was the same. The movement of the rudder bars under her feet was familiar. Her eyes scanned the interior. Each item, taken separately, seemed correct and in place. Yet everything had changed so drastically—so suddenly.

She looked entreatingly at her instructor strolling away and yearned to call him back—tell him she wasn't ready. Not yet. But on the other hand, she wanted desperately to take this next step and be convinced of her own ability—to become the pilot who lived, up to this point, only in her imagination.

Experimentally she pushed forward on the throttle— heard the engine respond and saw the tachometer change. The airplane remained motionless, however. One of the little wheels had found a depression in the sod so she continued to advance the throttle with, deliberate care, until she felt movement. Then she slowed the engine until a steady rate of travel was achieved. Surprisingly, the craft's behavior, under her control, seemed hardly changed by his absence. Her right and left pedal applications produced the same effect as before in steering the zigzag path needed to compensate for the lack of vision straight ahead.

At the end of the runway, near the fence, she turned off to the left into the space designated as the "run-up area". Here she depressed the right rudder bar fully and, with an extra surge of power from the engine, swung the tail of the airplane so that she faced crossways to the strip. As she progressed through the sequence of preflight checks, her confidence increased. Fuel: on, carburetor heat: off, oil pressure: between thirty and forty, oil temperature: above seventy-five, gas quantity: alright (the indicator rod, in front of the windshield, protruded from the cap about four inches).

Heels hard on the brakes, she set the engine speed at the recommended nineteen-hundred revolutions per minute and positioned the magneto switch to settings marked R, BOTH, L. BOTH while noting that the decrease on the tachometer was less than one-hundred r.p.m. Application of carburetor heat caused even less change. Satisfied, she brought the engine speed to idle.

The trim setting required a moment of deliberation. Let's see, she instructed herself. Without him in here, the weight in front is less so I should have it more "nose-down" than usual.

Control freedom was verified by moving the stick in a full circle and alternatey pressing the rudder bars.

Have I forgotten anything? she said to herself.

A last look around was needed for assurance, but then she felt the trembling start in her arms and legs. "Don't th . . . think about it!" The self-inflicted scolding failed to calm her. With a sigh of resignation, she continued with the final preparations.

Across the runway from her position, the windsock hung limp on it's mast confirming that wind-direction was not a factor to be considered. Dutifully she scanned the skies for other airplanes (which were never there) and then, with great trepidation, eased forward on the throttle.

The Cub rolled onto the strip and, seemingly having a mind of its own, aligned itself for takeoff. Katie quickly retarded the throttle and braked to a halt. Her teeth had started to chatter.

"D . . . d . . . damn!" she said aloud thinking she might get sick. Then she saw him through the left side arc of the propeller, standing off the runway halfway down its length. He ought to know if I can do it or not. She studied his posture for signs of concern. There didn't appear to be any. He stood watching, his weight over one leg, one hand in a pocket, the other holding a cigarette.

He must be crazy to trust me with his airplane. Her jaw muscles hardened. "Well God-dam . . . dammit!" she screamed aloud. "Either I'm a p . . . pil . . . pilot or I ain't!" She opened the throttle and released the brakes before she could change her mind.

The engine's roar seemed more pronounced. This startled her so that she was slow to apply adequate right rudder to counter the airplane's tendency to veer left. Then she corrected with too much pressure so that the fat little tires described parallel S's in the grass before she had full control. Forward stick brought the tail up and, unexpectedly, she was flying.

The craft rose at a rate that made her gasp. A quick glance at the indicator confirmed airspeed in excess of fifty miles per hour, but the long front section appeared to be pitched up at an astonishing angle. She quickly pushed the stick forward and, with the other hand, cranked the trim control to relieve the pressure. This brought about a more acceptable climb attitude to Katie's profound relief.

As she relaxed back in the seat, awareness struck her like a thunderbolt. "Wow!" she yelled. "Wow!" She burst into hysterical, shrieking laughter, giving herself over entirely to exhilaration and release. Tears streamed down her face. Joyfully she rocked the long wings from side to side. "Hey!" she shouted to the world below. "Look at me! L . . . look at m . . . me! I'm flying!"

The altimeter showed almost six-thousand feet before she sobered. Wiping her eyes on her sleeves, she reduced the engine power and turned back toward the field.

What must he be thinking? she wondered, suddenly concerned.

For an anxious minute she couldn't find the airfield until she realized that the plane's erratic meandering had taken her west of Benson Ward.

A thousand feet too high, she realized and reached for the carburetor heat control. With the throttle set for fifteen-hundred rpm, she began a long gliding return on a path that would bring her to the right side and parallel with the strip.

In her mind she rehearsed the landing procedure: Carburetor heat on—I already have it on—, five-thousand feet pattern altitude, chop the throttle opposite the touch-down point, glide speed of sixty miles per hour, check field for position, turn base, clear engine, turn final, reduce speed to fifty-five, clear engine, slip or add power as needed and, finally, flare for landing.

The airplane descended with agonizing slowness and was more than three-hundred feet high as it passed the point opposite the touchdown end of the landing strip.

I'll have to extend my downwind glide, Katie decided closing the throttle. "How far?" she voiced her concern, glancing anxiously over her left shoulder. Her voice sounded unnaturally loud with only the sound of rushing air outside the cabin and the gentle ticking of the engine.

"How f . . . far?" she said again.

Should be enough. With a touch of throttle, the engine roared for a brief moment, reassuringly. Katie adjusted the heading of the airplane perpendicular to a line she imagined extended from the runway and then turned to follow that line. The airspeed indicator showed sixty so she pulled with more pressure on the stick to slow the craft.

"The trim!" she admonished herself. "I forgot the tr . . . trim!"

A final burst of power to clear the engine and then she knew. "Oh no! Too h . . . high!"

She jabbed the right rudder bar and pushed the stick left. The airplane canted crazily but then settled into the forward slip attitude that brought about a sharp reduction in velocity. Katie eased the back-pressure on the stick to maintain airspeed and watched. fearfully, the approach of the tiny landing strip through the side window.

"Still t . . . t . . . too high!" she wailed as the field boundary passed more than a hundred feet below. The distance to the other end of the field was diminishing rapidly.

Go around! her consciousness screamed.

Reflexes, conditioned by the hours of instruction and repetition, took over. The engine responded to the application of full throttle and, after a momentary oscillation, the cub straightened and began climbing. Katie had a fleeting glimpse of Crow standing beside the runway, hands on hips, grinning widely. The grin had a settling effect on her rapidly decomposing confidence.

"Now, d . . . damn it!" she shouted. "Do it right!"

This time she executed her crosswind left turn at precisely forty-nine hundred feet and at five-thousand, turned downwind while reducing power to hold altitude. Flying parallel with the runway, she reached for the carburetor heat.

"Shit! Forgot to p . . . push it off."

As the end of the strip came even with her left wing, she pulled the throttle, noting with satisfaction that the altitude still showed five-thousand.

Now trim for sixty, she told herself while rotating the crank backwards until the plane would maintain the proper speed without pressure on the control stick.

There! Now let's go out a little further this time. She was using Crow's words for her thoughts and it was helping.

Okay! Turn here. The cub swung obediently.

Clear the engine and then turn on final. The craft surged forward with the momentary increase in power and began the final turn.

She thought she might be low. Wait and see, his words told her. Clear your engine and slow to fifty.

Then she was over the fence and applying back pressure on the stick to stop the descent.

"Hold it off!" he would be saying.

She complied, not letting the wheels touch until the airplane would no longer fly. Forward vision through the windshield was lost as the long snout lifted slowly upward so that Katie was left with only that directional and height information that could be gleaned looking through the side windows.

"Don't look down at the ground!" she could hear his warning. "Look past the nose."

She felt the hard resistance as the control stick reached the aft limit of its travel. And immediately afterwards, the wheels sank gratefully into the grass. Katie pumped the rudder bars to keep the craft rolling straight while holding the wings level with the stick until the speed had diminished to a slow wallowing crawl. At that point she applied full left rudder and, with a blast from the propeller, swung the airplane around on the strip to face in the opposite direction.

Taxing past her instructor, she threw him a quick, dazzling smile.

On the second landing, the Piper was too high above the surface when it quit flying and reacted with a bounce several feet up. This time the smile was somewhat strained.

Her final circuit produced a landing that was, to her immense relief, satisfactory. Not as good as the first, she decided, but okay.

Before entering the airplane, he stood for a long period in the turbulent air blowing from the propeller, looking at her. Wave after wave of emotions surged through her. The tears on her cheeks contrasted strangely with the bright smile showing through trembling lips.

"Alright pilot," he said at last. "Take me to the barn."

* * *

He leaned against the rough boards of the building and watched the girl as she pedaled the bicycle toward Smithfield. He caught occasional glimpses of her between trees that lined the road. She sat upright on the seat—back straight as a spar—slim and long-legged.

The harsh lines of his face had softened in keeping with his pensive mood. It was always like this after he had soloed a student. More so this time. In those moments the awful weight of responsibility descended upon him like a lead cloak. What would be the ultimate result of my involvement in her life? Have I placed her future in jeopardy?

Now she has flown, he thought, relying totally on her own skills and abilities to protect her. Master of her own fate, so to speak, and she likes it. No doubt about that. The look on her face told everything. She couldn't have put it into words—wouldn't, of course—but it was there. The look that said, "I did it! I willingly submitted myself to a really challenging situation that held an element of danger and, by my own hand, I prevailed."

He continued to stare at a point down the road where she had disappeared and tried to analyze his feelings. Why was it so much more important with this girl? Was it compassion? Pity?

Or, he wondered, is it just my nature to root for the underdog?

Certainly she was a most unlikely pilot. Yet, because she was so bright and quick, with such an overwhelming desire to fly, her progress had been well above average. Already she had surpassed some of the young men who had begun training earlier. Nevertheless he felt that he had been severely tested as an instructor with Katie. Oddly enough, it wasn't in a technical sense. She seemed to have a fair degree of mechanical aptitude, in spite of her youth, and this surprised him. The women he knew showed very little interest in engines and other mechanisms. Only a relative few drove automobiles. But he knew Katie was different. On several Sunday mornings she had arrived early and happily lent a hand servicing the Cub. She had strong, dexterous fingers that could perform some tasks he found difficult with his own stubby digits.

It was in communicating with the girl that he had to be very resourceful. If she could talk, what a world-beater she would be, he pondered. But with her, communications is a one-way street.

No, that isn't exactly true, he reminded himself. She does communicate, but in subtle ways. After all the time he had spent with the girl, he'd reached the point where he could almost hear her thoughts as if she'd spoken. The position of her shoulders, or the lift of her chin gave voice to her moods. He could read words in the widening of her eyes or the set of her mouth or the tilt of her head. She would look at him with those intelligent eyes and he would know she understood everything he was saying. Especially in the beginning, he had tried to express himself using the simplest terms in describing the most elementary concepts. Finally he had come to realize that it wasn't necessary.

But how far can she go? he pondered. As time passes, two-way radios will become more common for communications between airplanes and ground stations. Small airplanes will have radios someday—might even be required. Then what would Katie do? She'll never use a transmitter. And if she couldn't . . . ?

He remained for a considerable period of time staring fixedly in the direction she had taken. "My God!" he said at last. "What have I done?"

Chapter 13

As she hoed in the cornfield, Katie sang the Friml/Hammerstein song, "Indian Love Call" from "Rose-Marie", trying to sound like Jeanette Macdonald.

"When I'm calling you -ooo-ooo.
Will you answer true -ooo-ooo?"

She changed from a soprano voice to a Nelson Eddy baritone.

"That means I offer my love to you,
To be your own.
If you refuse me I will be blue,
And waiting all alone."

Once again her baritone became a soprano.

"But if when you hear,
My love call ringing clear.
And I hear your answering echo so dear."

Not able to mimic the dual harmonizing voices of the two, she settled for Jeanette:

"Then I will know our love . . ."

She stopped singing when she heard Bart's car drive into the field with his dog, Duke, sitting beside him. He motioned her over to the car and yelled, "Bring your stuff. You won't be back today."

Katie returned to the ditch bank and picked up her file, water-jug, bag of books, hat and shoes. She walked to the car, put her belongings behind the seat and pushed the dog over to make room.

Bart started the car moving. "I've leased a pasture from Jed Olsen out toward Almalga." Want to keep the grass behind the barn for the cows." He took a quick glance at the girl. "How you coming on the corn?"

"F . . . fine."

"Looked like you was about half done. Didn't your ma get after you for not wearing shoes?" The big man showed a grin.

Katie returned the grin.

"Well, you better put 'em on now that you're going to be chasing livestock," he said. "You'll wear out your feet on them graveled roads. Duke will be a little help but sometimes he gets over excited."

Katie petted the dog.

"When we get to your place, take your stuff out and then meet me at the pasture gate." He drove in silence until he pulled up in front of the Stuart house.

Katie slipped on her shoes and took the other items to the house. Then she walked over to the pasture gate.

"We'll get 'em collected here before we turn 'em out. Sadie and Peaches are over there." He pointed. "Get them first. Take Duke and take his ball." He tossed her the ball. "Just throw the ball where you want him to go."

The girl and the dog went out in the pasture and drove the two heifers back to the gate. When they returned, Bart gave further instructions. "Now get Melba and the two steers. I'll hold these here."

Katie and Duke rounded up the rest of the stock and drove them to the gate.

"Hold 'em here and I'll go open the gate," Bart told the girl."

When the gate was opened, Katie and Duke drove the cattle through and out to the road. "I'll drive behind 'em," Bart said. "You try to keep 'em on the road."

For the next hour the girl and the dog ran almost constantly. The cattle were determined to be anywhere except on the road. They had to be chased out of peoples' yards, out of lanes that led into barnyards and out of fields where gates had been left open. Katie was constantly climbing through fences and racing across fields to head off the stock that invariably turned onto the wrong road. She carried Duke's ball and when she saw that the animals were getting ahead of her on a side road, she'd throw the ball. Duke would bound over a fence and land in front of the started cows.

About the time Katie was ready to drop from exhaustion, Bart yelled, "That's it up ahead. Hold 'em and I'll go through and open the gate." He drove carefully past the cattle as Katie threw rocks at any that tried to double back.

Finally the five animals were safely corralled inside the pasture. Bart and his two fatigued drovers got into the car. He looked at the girl. "I don't remember hearing you use that kind of language before."

Katie scowled and the big man laughed. "Cows tend to bring out the worst in people." He reached into his pocket and pulled out two dollar coins. "A little something extra."

Katie happened to look skyward and saw the Piper Cub passing. She clutched the coins in her hand and smiled—a very secret smile.

Chapter 14

After the Sunday morning flying lesson, they had taken to sitting on an old wooden bench, in the warm sunshine, where they could look at the Cub. Katie's reluctance to ask questions, placed on her instructor the burden of trying to anticipate problems she was having with the training program.

He suspected that the questions she might have asked, were those he had heard many times before from other students—some were his own questions from the days of primary flight training in the "Jennys". He reiterated those items of information that he felt were vital, hoping that she would retain the knowledge if she heard it stated differently or in another context.

"One of the major distinctions between driving a car and flying a plane has to do with speed," he'd told her after the first lesson. "If you're driving and get yourself into a pinch, you probably want less speed. The faster you're going when you hit something, the worse it hurts. Therefore, you'd probably use your brakes to get yourself out of trouble—in other words, reduce your speed.

"In the air, you have to turn your thinking around. Too slow is real trouble. You've got to keep that wing lifting. If it quits on you anywhere between ten feet and a thousand feet above the ground, you're going to have an interesting time.

The only way that wing is going to do its job is to be pulled through the air fast enough. In the Cub, that means fifty miles per hour, or better. I told you before, it stalls at about forty but you'd better allow for a ten mile per hour margin for error, at least. Otherwise you could end up, someday, with grass in your teeth."

Once, after she had a particularly difficult time with landings, he had accused her of being afraid of the ground.

"Get down close," he'd told her. "Don't be scared of touching down before you've lost flying speed. As long as you're in a landing attitude, it's okay. Just continue your flare—keep coming back on the stick. If the plane contacts the ground and then lifts off again, don't worry. Even if it happens two or three times. The trick is to stay close to the ground. That way, when the wing stalls, you don't have far to drop. It's the 'drop' that could ruin your day.

"The same holds true for emergency landings out in the boondocks. Pick the best open area you can see for landing into the wind. If you have enough altitude, try to fly a normal pattern but stay a little high. Slip the airplane to slow it down or lose altitude. Then get down close to the ground, whether it's a pasture, sagebrush or somebody's bean patch. Most important, don't let the ground scare you, not even if you're going into trees. You'll save your skin if you fly it at minimum glide speed right down to the ground. If there's trees, try to steer between 'em. Let the trees shear the wings off. That will absorb some of the energy."

Usually he talked to her until his next student arrived. Quite often she stayed on for a second lesson in the afternoon. As a result, she learned who were her fellow Sunday flyers.

Will Fletcher, his friend Dwaine Parkins and Bing Bingstrom she knew from North Cache High. Tweet Anderson, from the south end of the valley, had his lessons later in the afternoon but sometimes came early just to watch the activity. Bob Garrett, who lived in Logan, she saw only a couple of times. Several had lessons on other days and didn't come around often on Sundays.

The instructor stood when they heard a car driving in. "That'll be Dwaine," Crow said. Shortly after the sound of car doors slamming reached them, Dwaine and Will came around the corner of the building.

Will, his usual jolly self, greeted the instructor. "Hello Crow. Whatta' you know? Hi, Katie. Glad to see you didn't crash today so we've still got an airplane to fly."

Will giggled as Dwaine pounded his upper arm. "Hi Katie," he said. "Don't pay any attention to this knothead. He just likes to hear his mouth flap. You can probably fly circles around him."

"Well you know how it is with lady pilots?"

Dwaine looked at his friend. "How's that?"

"They're always flyin' of the handle. Hee hee hee."

Crow shook his head watching Will. "Is he always like this?"

"Usually worse," Dwaine said. "When you get him up there today, push him out of the plane. He's so full of hot air, he won't fall. He'll just be floating over the valley until the wind blows him away."

Everyone laughed.

"That's enough chit chat," the instructor said. "We'd better get to it. I've got Bing and Tweet coming in later. Maybe Bob will show up after that. Who's first?"

"I'll flip you for it," Will said to Dwaine.

Dwaine pushed his friend toward the plane. "Go ahead. I'll keep Katie company."

Katie began walking toward her bicycle. "Uh huh. G . . .got . . . gotta' go."

A few minutes later, the plane passed her on takeoff as she rode along the road. She saw Will and Crow wave to her, and she waved back.

Sure don't want to be alone with Dwaine, she said to herself. Never know what might happen. He might try to take advantage of me. She laughed aloud.

Just how would he do that? Della and Georgina made it seem like a girl could get seduced just by walking past him. She giggled at the thought.

Opal's probably right. People make up stories. Just because he's good-looking, they think he's getting into the pants of every girl he's seen with. That's silly. Not every girl is Shelly or Zelma. I'll bet most of those in school are virgins—even Della and Georgina. They just talk big and Opal would pee her pants if Dwaine ever made a move on her.

Katie laughed aloud. I would too, she thought, except I don't have to worry. He'd never be much interested in Stutterin' Stuart—no guy would. I'm surprised he even talks to me. Hell, I'm surprised he even knows my name. But then, I think he's nice to everybody.

Chapter 15

Bart Johnson brought his tractor to a stop in front of the Stuart home. "Howdy," he called to Clara, who was seated on her front porch. "Home safe and sound again."

"God evening, Mister Johnson," the woman replied.

Katie slid off the hay wagon, that was hitched to the tractor, taking her straw hat and a bag.

"Here you go, gal," Johnson said as he flipped a dollar coin to the girl."

Katie dropped her bag and caught the coin with a free hand. "Th . . . thanks."

"That's very nice of you to be paying her a dollar a day," Clara said.

"She earns it," Bart said. "I pay her what she's worth and she's worth one hell of a lot" The big man took off his hat and wiped his forehead with the sleeve of his shirt. "She does the work of half a dozen kids. Why should I pay a bunch of lazy little bastards two-bits a piece to stomp all over my crops?"

He put the tractor in gear and drove off yelling, "See you tomorrow, Katie."

"That man uses the worst language of anyone I know." Clara's face showed her disgust. "You can hear him all over town."

Katie climbed the stairs and sat on the porch. Clara studied her daughter. "You look like a bum dressed like that. Those slacks are at least six inches too short and I don't know where you got that old blouse. Why do you tie it in front like that?"

"C . . . cool . . . er."

'You're not wearing that hat when you work, are you? Your face is so brown you look like an Indian. Don't you know too much sun is bad for you?"

Katie shrugged and looked out at the street. Says the same thing every night, she thought.

Her mother released a sigh. "Well, you're not going to listen to me, are you? I might as well talk to a stone wall.

Katie juggled the dollar coin in her hand.

Clara took notice. "Now that you're earning some money, what are you going to do with it? You ought to be able to buy some nice clothes and accessories."

"D ... d ... don't need any ... thing." Katie glanced at her mother.

Clara showed her exasperation. "I guess it's up to you if you don't want to look nice."

Mother and daughter sat quietly for a period of time. Finally Clara spoke again. "By the way, they're playing 'Rose Marie' with Jeanette Macdonald and Nelson Eddy at the Main. Do you want to go?"

"S ... sure. Are you p ... payin'?"

"Yes," Clara said, annoyed. "I'm paying. She stood and started inside. "Well come on and get cleaned up before dinner."

Chapter 16

The morning had been windy and Katie worried that it would be too much for the light Cub.

"No, it's going to be alright," Crow told her after observing the windsock for a moment. "You need some wind experience. We'll put this little ol' breeze to good use before it gets too busy."

They made quick preflight preparations and started the engine. As they taxied toward the runup area, he showed her special tricks for ground handling an airplane in the wind. One problem that became apparent to Katie, while taxing downwind, was trying to prevent the airplane from turning into the wind.

"It wants to act just like a big weather vane," he explained.

The reason for holding the stick full forward, with the craft facing away from the wind, was emphasized by her instructor.

"If the wind, coming from behind, gets under the elevators, it's going to flip this bird over on its back. You're going to find yourself hanging upside down by your safety belt and I'm going to have an expensive repair bill."

Airborne, she performed crosswind "S" turns over a road and quickly became familiar with the need for wide, extended turns made while flying upwind as compared with the more abrupt turns made while flying downwind.

Later he demonstrated a crosswind landing approach to a mowed hay field, stressing the degree to which the airplane had to be turned toward the wind in order that their track over the ground remained aligned with their intended landing strip. Several attempts were needed for her to master the technique. Drifting sideways with the wind was a new sensation—quite different from that caused by deliberately crossing controls to make the airplane slip.

He'd told her earlier that it was the same as crossing a river in a boat. "If you point the boat directly across the river, you'll reach the other side some distance downstream, depending on the current. To go straight across, you have to angle the boat upstream enough to compensate for the flow."

Katie also learned that the airplane's alignment, with its track over the ground, could be held in a crosswind if the upwind wing was lowered such that the resulting sideslip rate matched the wind's velocity.

By the time they returned to the home field, the windsock was being blown almost perpendicular to the mast. This brought about Katie's introduction to the "wheel landing".

"Fifteen-hundred on the tach," he told her, "and fly it level onto the ground. Land on the main gear with the tail high."

The plane's speed seemed hardly faster than she could run as it crossed the boundary fence and skimmed the grass. When she felt the tires touch, quick forward pressure on the stick, as directed, held the wheels on the ground while the throttle was pulled and the tail settled. The wheel landing seemed easier to Katie than the three-point landing with the wing in a full stall configuration.

"Don't plan on a second lesson today," he told Katie as they tied the Cub securely to anchors, fastened to blocks buried under the turf. "It's turning into a pretty good blow."

They settled themselves on the bench and he told her about wheel landings. "That Cub should be wheel landed only on long runways or into stiff winds."

She was, again, amazed that he knew what she was thinking. "Wheel landings seem almost too easy after full stall landings," he explained, "especially if you make a good one on your first try. But let me tell you something. If you botch up a wheel landing, either by not carrying enough power and speed, or by trying to force the airplane onto the ground, you'll think you've got a wildcat by the tail. The first thing it will do is jump up higher than this building and then, if you're not quick enough to catch it with power, it'll probably stall and give you another hard bounce."

Just about the time she decided never again to try a wheel landing, he grinned at her with his crinkled face.

"Now I don't want to scare you—I just want you to realize that you can't use a wheel landing as a bail out. You should become proficient with many forms of flying under a variety of conditions so you can handle anything. And that includes wheel landings."

* * *

When Dwaine Parkins arrived, she retrieved her bicycle and started for home. For a while, she pedaled into the increasing wind, but soon tired. She was walking, pushing the bicycle, when the sound of gravel, crunching under tires behind, gave her a start.

"You look like someone who could use a lift." Dwaine smiled at her from inside the Pontiac.

She returned the smile but shook her head.

"It's alright," he assured her. "We can put your bike in the back. You'll be a week walking to Smithfield."

Still she hesitated, apprehensive, but he was already out of the car and opening the rumble seat. He took the bicycle from her yielding hands, lifted it overhead with ease and set it carefully inside the opening.

"Don't ever get in that car . . ."

She remembered the high school girl's warning but then there seemed no graceful way to decline.

How can I say no, she thought, without sounding like a goon. Besides, it's daytime. What could possibly happen, she asked herself. And he certainly seems nice enough, smiling his bashful little boy smile and opening the door for me to enter.

"I should have listened to Will," he said as they started out. "He told me it would be too windy. You're lucky you had your lesson before it got too bad, especially after riding all the way from Smithfield."

Katie nodded and looked, with careful nonchalance, about the interior of the car. How many other girls have been in here, she thought. Sitting and maybe something else.

"I was scheduled for a solo cross-country but Crow figured I'd get blown out of the state today." He glanced at her and smiled again.

She smiled back. My hair must look a mess, she thought. Self-consciously she pulled back her shoulders and raised her chin, aware that he was studying her.

"It's a little surprising that a girl would be interested in taking flying lessons," he said, finally. "Will and I are naturally a little shy on good sense, but what's your excuse?"

"It's fun." She thanked God there was no stutter.

"Good enough!" he said, chuckling. "Are you going to be another Amelia Earhart? That's what she said."

She looked at him with one eyebrow lifted, hoping she did it just right.

"I think there's still time for you to be the first woman to fly solo around the world," he said. "How about it?"

Katie giggled, shaking her head.

He was silent on the drive through Benson Ward so she contented herself with watching the quiet Sunday community pass by. Secretly she hoped to catch sight of some North Cache girls.

Boy! Would their eyes pop out of their heads, she thought. They'd be talking all next year—wondering if I was one of Dwaine's girls.

He caught her playing with her hand in the wind that whipped past the open window. "What's our airspeed?" he asked. "Heading into this wind, we must be doing eighty."

She grinned, sheepishly. Crow must be telling all his students the same things, she thought.

Before reaching the Bear River bridge, he turned to her. "Are you in a hurry to get home?"

She shrugged, not knowing how to respond to the question.

"I've got to stop in Amalga. Will's loaning me his horse trailer."

Katie nodded. What's he want with a horse trailer, she wondered.

Soon after passing the yellow brick church of Amalga Ward, she caught sight of the Bear River, again, as it swept in from the right. The slough along it's edge, bordered with cattails, marked the channel that the river had taken some time in the distant past.

Seeing the brown river where it began to curve in a giant arc around the old Amalgamated Sugar factory, she was reminded of her first flight in the Cub. The smokestack stood as a huge pylon overlooking the green countryside.

I'm going to come out here and fly around it again, she thought.

She let her eyes scan the panoramic view through the car windows and come to rest, for a brief moment, on the driver.

He sure is good-looking, she said to herself. No wonder the girls get silly around him. I'd never do that.

His shirt-sleeves were rolled up tight on muscular brown arms. Dark curly hair topped a rather narrow face with wideset brown eyes. The slight hollows in his cheeks and an aquiline nose gave him an appearance that was, as Opal described, "aristocratic".

When he turned and smiled, she felt her face flush.

"Just ahead," he pointed.

She wrinkled her nose at the smell as they passed the Amalga pea vinery. Then, a little further on, he turned into the farmyard. With an ease that Katie envied, he backed the car next to the trailer at the side of the barn.

She caught sight of Will in the corral, currying a sorrel. The horse appeared under -sized next to the massive youth.

Dwaine left the car and strode to the corral. Placing both hands on the top rail, he vaulted over.

She watched the two young men as they stood talking, one on each side of the horse. Will looked over at her and waved. Katie waved back.

I hope he doesn't come over to the car, she thought. People are always ready to think the worst.

She was beginning to feel uneasy being seen with Dwaine. And she was almost sure she caught Will winking at his friend.

After several minutes, Dwaine returned. She felt the car shutter as he attached the trailer. Then he was sitting beside her again and the car was rolling out onto the road, with the trailer rattling behind.

"My mare has to go to stud tomorrow," he announced. "Taking her over to Clarkston. There's a dandy Arabian I want to put her with."

She blushed, shocked at the matter-of-fact way he talked of such things. As a farm girl, Katie certainly had seen animals breeding but this was a subject that was not discussed around young ladies. Even Bart, who's normal language was guaranteed to disperse a gathering of Relief Society ladies within seconds, was extremely circumspect in talking with Katie about anything having to do with sex.

Dwaine drove slowly, glancing frequently at the rear view mirror. When they reached the church, he turned off onto the narrow road that led to the dismantled sugar factory.

"I'd better take it kinda easy with this thing," he explained with a jerk of his thumb indicating the trailer. "We'll take the back way to Smithfield."

As they passed the ruins of the factory, she leaned her head out the window to see the top of the smokestack. Yellow brick had been used in its construction and piles of brick rubble marked the location of other demolished facilities. A long warehouse and three small buildings were all that remained standing in the vicinity of the towering chimney.

"Really stands up there, doesn't it?" she heard him say.

She nodded and continued to watch with some apprehension. Their movement added to the illusion that the tall structure was toppling. She breathed easier when they were safely past.

"There's some climbing rungs set in the bricks inside that ol' chimney," he told her. "Go all the way to the top. Lew Wilson said he climbed up and sat on the rim. Can you imagine that?" Dwaine laughed and shook his head. "When I get that high off the ground, I want to be in an airplane."

He turned onto the road that took them down to the river bottoms. Soon they were clattering across a rickety, wooden bridge. Katie spotted three small boys playing among the willows growing on an island that had formed in the swirling, muddy river under the bridge. A little shelter—perhaps a fort to guard against attacking Indians—had been constructed by the boys using the willows. They waved at her and she waved back.

How did they get down there? Probably climbed down from the bridge, she decided. She'd heard that the river was too dangerous for swimming. "Whirlpools that'll take you right to the bottom and hold you there," they'd said.

The road led upward from the river and turned toward town. Katie was enjoying the ride immensely. The wind that earlier had whipped across the fields, raising dust, was gone. All her young senses were tuned, with exquisite fineness, to the summer's touch, to discovery and to the excitement brought about by the presence of the handsome man at her side.

She felt like singing, like yelling, like running and dancing. Instead she smiled at him.

"How about an apple?" he said, returning her smile.

Her look showed curiosity.

"Somebody planted an apple tree way out here in the fields. I'll show you."

As they rounded a bend, she saw where the road broke off to the left, toward town. He steered the car onto the lesser, winding road that led into a wooded area and off on a grassy lane. Then the car stopped and he was out. She turned and saw him bend to examine the trailer hitch before coming around to her side.

"Right over here," he said, opening the door.

She held back, frowning.

"Don't worry, it's Sunday. Owners aren't around," he assured her. "They don't care anyway."

He led her through a thicket of scrub trees and bushes. When he stopped, she looked up and saw the tree, heavy with variegated fruit.

"Best apples in the valley," he studied the tree. "Look ripe."

None were within reach so he pulled himself up into the tree and tossed down several for her to catch.

"May as well take some home," he said, climbing down. "They'll just go to rot."

Taking one of the apples, he settled down with his back against the trunk of the tree and began eating. The apples were, indeed, delicious, she soon discovered.

"Hold it," he cautioned as she looked around for a place to sit. "You'll get grass stains all over your slacks. Let me get something."

He returned shortly and threw the blanket, carelessly, next to the tree. "There, you'll have something to lean against."

They sat, side by side, happily chewing the succulent fruit. He pulled out a large, red handkerchief and, teasingly, dabbed at the little stream that had started down her chin. Giggling, she drew the back of her hand across her mouth.

She delighted in the tingling sensation on her skin where his leg rested against hers and again where their shoulders touched.

"That's a nice smile you've got there, kid." he told her. "Bet there's a gang of guys hot on your trail."

Katie looked at him directly, trying to determine if he was serious. She hoped he wasn't making fun of her.

"You got a boyfriend?"

She shook her head and looked away.

"Come on now. You're pullin' my leg. A good-lookin' kid like you?" His elbow was nudging her in the side. "How are you beatin' 'em off?"

She knew her face was getting red—could feel the prickling heat in her neck. How desperately she wanted to make a lighthearted, witty reply, with the same self-assurance she had envied in others.

She could sense his eyes on her. His frank examination brought on an overwhelming desire to be better—shorter with a full figure and longer, more curly hair.

"You've got a lot goin' for you, kid," she heard him say. "Really, you have. You're different . . ." He noticed that she stiffened at the word "different" and he quickly added, ". . . but in good ways. You're not like those other girls at North Cache who figure all they have to be, in this world, is cute and giggly. All they think about is their hair and clothes and makeup and getting married. That's all they talk about, too. A fellow gets awfully tired of that."

She liked his voice. It wasn't harsh and brittle—certainly not like the voice of his friend, Will—but low and soft. He didn't speak the "farm dialect", either. His talk was more like the teachers, with good diction and pronunciation.

"You're more serious," he went on. "I noticed it at school. Matter-of-fact, I noticed quite a lot about you."

She looked at him, disbelieving, her mouth twisted and one eyebrow lifted.

A burst of laughter exploded from the young man at her side. "Honest to God!" he said. "It would take a book to describe what you can do with one expression. But it's true. I never had much of a chance getting to know you. I guess it was because you seemed so . . . ," he searched for a word, ". . . aloof. I figured you wouldn't give me the time of day."

Aloof! she thought, incredulously. Me, aloof! She laughed and shook her head.

"You were!" he protested. "You always seemed to be studying—even outside the school. You gave the impression you didn't want anyone bothering you. That's what I meant about 'serious'. All that silliness you left to the other girls. I admired you for that. You've got substance."

Could that really be true? Katie wondered. Is that the impression I give everyone? Maybe if I wasn't so serious, I wouldn't have all these problems."

His words penetrated her thoughts. With the bashful smile, that she was finding irresistible, he was telling her how much he liked her ears. "I'm an ear man," he said. "For some strange reason I'm attracted to girls who have nicely formed little ears."

He laughed at her look of disbelief.

"Maybe it's because I have this pair of barn doors hanging on the side of my head. Pa says if I wiggle 'em fast enough, I should be able to fly without an airplane."

He caught her looking at his ears and laughed again, causing her to blush furiously and turn away.

His ears aren't too big, she thought. He's just teasing and I shouldn't be acting like such a dummy.

But when he reached over and delicately traced the outline of her ear, Katie thought she would jump out of her skin. Giggling, she pushed him away. He rolled over on his side in an exaggerated, slow-motion tumble, his legs held high at awkward angles. With a great amount of feigned effort and groaning he brought himself upright beside her.

"If you don't cut out the rough stuff," he told her, "you'll never have any boyfriends."

She slapped playfully at him and he caught her hand.

"See? There you go again," he admonished her. "You've got to bring that vicious streak under control."

Katie's full attention was focused on her hand being held in his, so that she found herself unable to concentrate on his words. She smiled with the pleasure of his touch and the wondrous feelings she was experiencing.

He looked steadily at her face for a time. "Lovely eyes," he said at last. "Somewhere between light gray and blue, set apart the way eyes should be."

Still holding her hand and looking into her eyes, he moved closer. "You probably won't believe this about me, either, but I've made a study of eyes. It's those people with shifty little eyes, close together, that you've got to watch out for. They can be mean and vicious. But these eyes aren't mean. They're not vicious. A little sad at times. A little discouraged once in a while. These are good eyes. And they're intelligent eyes. These eyes want to see things and know things. They're not content to be just another pair of eyes. The eyes I'm looking at belong to a person who will do something with her life—be somebody. That person will not be content with what she is now, but try to be a whole lot more.

"Now I may not know much, but I do know about eyes. It's a feeling I have inside me. And yours are special eyes."

Katie sat solemnly looking at him—listening as he spoke quietly, telling about her very soul and she felt the sting of tears starting.

He drew her to him and gently kissed the tears on her cheeks. She felt as if she had been waiting forever for someone to talk to her as he was doing. An overwhelming tenderness for him welled up inside her. She wanted to thank him in a thousand ways for giving her that special glow of attractiveness. Suddenly nothing mattered more than to give him pleasure and she turned to him, eagerly, when his lips brushed her hair.

And because she was very young, she couldn't understand the emotions that betrayed her, blocking out all reason; was not acquainted with the urgings that had taken control of her body; knew no restraints that could divert the course of events from its design.

When awareness came, with the realization of what had happened to her, Katie was overcome with shock and a sad sense of loss. She turned away from Dwaine's gaze as the flow of tears began.

Dwaine stared in disbelief at her bare back as she sat on the blanket sobbing, her body trembling. The appeal of this girl had him confused. He had made love with a number of young women in the past, but this was the first time he had been truly ashamed afterwards. The urge to hold and comfort her was also something new. "I'm sorry, kid," he said quietly. "I'm sorry. I shouldn't have been the one—not me!"

She could feel his eyes on her as she pulled on her clothes and walked away toward the car.

On the drive to Smithfield she huddled, miserable and humiliated, on the corner of the seat against the door. She wondered if she could stop the crying before she reached home and came under her mother's scrutiny.

Chapter 17

All that week, in the potato field, she thought of little else other than Sunday's occurrence.

What if I'm pregnant? How will I know? She considered the consequence of her mother finding out and the thought almost made her sick to her stomach.

At times she would stand, leaning on her hoe, staring at the blue hills and trying to analyze how it could have happened.

That was the first time I've ever been held that way by a man, she thought. First time I've been kissed that way, too. She remembered his whiskers scratching her face and was amazed that she didn't seem to care. And when he was removing her clothes and touching her body, she didn't want him to stop.

So that's how it's done, she thought wonderingly. I didn't even know how, but it happened anyway. Was it that way with those other girls? Were they that easy? How did they feel afterward? Cheap? Used?

I certainly had plenty of warning so I can't say I didn't know better, she scolded herself, remembering remarks she had overheard at school. Should never have gotten in that car with him.

She worried, too, that the experience had altered her appearance in some way. Can people tell if you've done it? She tried to picture Shelly and see what was different about her as compared with some of the other girls. Was it the mouth? The eyes? The way she held herself?

That Sunday evening, and every evening since it happened, she had studied her reflection in the bathroom mirror, searching for the revealing evidence.

How come everyone at school knows who the girls are that have done it? That thought plagued her relentlessly. Those are the girls with the "reputations"—like Shelly. It was rumored at North Cache that, in her sophomore year, she had been one of Dwaine's girls. I suppose they'll know me, too, Katie chided herself viciously. Just another Shelly! Another of Dwaine's girls.

The word "reputation" repeated itself over and over in her mind. The idea that she had become a "fallen woman" both appalled and intrigued her. She pictured herself in a slinky, long, black dress, her hair piled high in a magnificent coiffure, a bejeweled cigarette holder, of enormous length, between her fingers, standing with hand on hip and saying (in a distinctively sultry, nasal tone of voice), If ya want it, big boy, ya know where ya can find it.

In the back of her mind she could hear Cole Porter's song "Love For Sale".

"Love for sale.
Appetizing young love for sale.
Love that's fresh and still unspoiled,
Love that's only slightly soiled.
Love for sale."

Maybe I should have named a price, she thought savagely.

At times, there were tears of anger directed at Dwaine, that he could have taken advantage of her ignorance.

What a smooth talking bastard, she recalled. He should be, of course. He's had plenty of practice. All that crap about my ears and eyes. How could I ever fall for that? I must be really dumb! God! Were you a pushover! she told herself, accusingly. Perfect set of round heels. He didn't even have to work at it.

She wondered if all his other girls had been that easy and she hated him. But then she remembered his gentleness, the sweet things he said, his strong arms holding her, his sympathy. She remembered, also, his anguish and self-recriminations on that long ride home.

Why blame him? she asked herself, finally. He just took what was offered up. My God! I practically threw myself at him!

Nevertheless, she was sure of one thing—she never wanted to see him again. Wouldn't dare, she confessed. Still, there seemed no way to avoid him unless she just stopped flying.

And Katie quickly rejected that idea.

* * *

"With a small engine at this altitude," he was telling her, "your airplane needs all the help it can get."

Katie had wanted to leave as soon after her lesson as she could, without seeming impolite, but Crow wanted to talk. She'd decided against waiting for an afternoon lesson.

"You take a real hot day, that Cub isn't going to climb worth a damn, especially carrying two big people. Hell, it might not even get off the ground, or it may lift up a couple of feet and just float there, ready to mow down a corn field.

When the air's hot, it gets thin—just like at high altitude. It cuts down engine power and reduces your wing lift. You have to keep that in mind when you're operating out of short fields, like this one on warm days."

Katie tried to present a calm, attentive demeanor but inside, she was churning with agitation. Please stop talking, she prayed inside.

"Now to get out of long grass or mud or snow, especially with thin air, you want to keep the tail low, but not touching the ground, during the takeoff run. That way the wing will start trying to pull the wheels up out of the muck as soon as you get moving."

He looked at her carefully. "Are you with me?"

Startled, she nodded quickly.

"Okay," he went on, "provided you get off the ground, you've still got to get some altitude. If the plane doesn't want to climb, don't force it. The tendency is to pull back harder on the stick. Don't do it or you're going to stall and make a yellow scrap pile out of my Piper. Just fly it close to the ground until it's ready to go up. You'll get some help from the ground. It's called 'ground effect'. At the same time, you'll want to make gentle turns to follow the lowest terrain and avoid obstructions.

"Now if you were trying to get over those mountains," he pointed east, "there's a couple other tricks you ought to know about. Here is where you can help your airplane with a little planning. You must have read about this in one of your books, but let me remind you. When the wind is blowing against a mountain, the air rises, following the surface upward."

He emphasized his words with hand motions. "You can fly in this area of rising air and get a lot of free lift. That ol' Cub will really go upstairs. Just like an elevator."

Katie shook herself, mentally, to maintain her concentration.

"So if you just keep track of wind direction, you can make it work for you. Of course if you guess wrong," he grinned at her, "you're going to have a close look at a lot of rocks and trees because the air is moving downward on the side of the mountain away from the wind."

When they heard the car drive up, Crow stood and stretched, indicating the lecture had ended. Katie rose and, with a contrived, casual air, sauntered inside the building. Making her way into the office she peered cautiously through the window and saw Dwaine walk past. When she heard him greet the instructor, she opened the door. A quick glance confirmed that he was around the corner, out of sight.

"Well hi ya there, gal!"

She jumped at the sound of his voice—surprised. Will's roar of laughter shattered the summer calm. He was sitting in the Pontiac with the door open holding a bottle of beer.

"I didn't mean to make you pee your pants. Hee! hee! hee!" His voice raised an octave with the giggle.

Katie laughed, mirthlessly, and moved toward her bicycle.

"Hey! What's the big rush?" he asked wiping his eyes with big thumbs. "Why don't ya stick around for a while? I've gotta wait for m'lesson til Dwaine's done. Company'd be nice.

She shook her head, smiling, and pulled her bicycle away from the building.

"Aw come on, now! My ol' man says I gotta face that'd stop a train—and probably had—but he tends to exaggerate."

He was out of the car, by this time, walking beside her. "I usually don't scare the girls quite that bad."

She giggled, then, as much for the comical face he made as for his remarks.

He gestured toward the bicycle. "Long way to ride that thing, isn't it?"

She shrugged.

"How about me takin' you home in Dwaine's car while he's up flyin'?" He closed one eye in a slow wink. "We could stop off for some apples."

She whirled on him—aghast.

"Hey, wait a minute!" He recoiled from the look on her face. "I ain't so bad. Gimme a break!"

Stunned, she didn't see Dwaine approach.

"Hey Katie!"

Quickly she turned and began pushing the bicycle toward the road.

"Katie!" He hurried to catch up with her. "What's the matter?"

She stopped and faced him with a look that was deadly. "You t . . . t . . . told!"

Then her face crumbled, reflecting the hurt and disillusion of all the world's betrayed women. "Y . . . y . . . you told!" she sobbed.

He stood, helpless, as she turned and ran, pushing the bicycle on the road.

"What the hell did you say to her?" he yelled at Will.

"Now hold on!" The big youth bristled, momentarily, then relaxed, grinning. "I didn't know I was cuttin' in on somethin' special."

Dwaine shook his head, impatiently. "What did you say?" he demanded.

Will spread his hands. "Christ, Dwaine! I didn't say nothin' 'cept maybe she might want to share the wealth."

"What! I told you nothing happened."

"Well, since you stopped for your favorite apples," Will said lamely, "I assumed . . ."

As he watched his friend's face darken with anger and saw his hands close into hard fists, Will remembered, uneasily, what he had seen happen to Mel Farnley.

Standing almost nose to nose with the other, Dwaine showed that same fury. "God damn it, Will!" he hissed through clenched teeth, "She's no pig! She's a nice kid! You leave her alone! I'm only going to tell you once!"

Will stood in amazement as his friend turned and stalked off toward the airplane. "Jeezus!" he muttered to himself. "Him 'n Stuttern' Stuart!"

Chapter 18

Even before she introduced herself, he knew, with a certain uneasiness, who she was. The facial features were the same. He was looking at the woman Katie would become in about twenty years.

She was tall and well formed with short hair, a shade darker than her daughter's. He noted the same serious, wideset eyes and the direct manner with which she regarded him.

"Crowther Spencer," he said offering his hand. If she smiled, he thought, I bet it would be Katie's smile.

But Clara Stuart wasn't smiling. They stood, taking each other's measure, for a moment. Then, remembering his manners, he quickly dusted off a rickety chair and offered it to her, apologetically.

"Be careful of that thing. It's seen better days."

On her precarious perch, she continued her evaluation of the pilot, obviously puzzled.

"I didn't hear you drive up." He had to say something.

"I had a heck of a time finding this place." She seemed equally relieved that the conversation was starting off in safe territory. "I drove by twice before I saw the airplane. Andrew told me you were off the Benson Ward road, but that's all."

His eyebrows lifted. "Andrew?"

This brought a frown from the woman. "Andrew Bingstrom!" she said, firmly.

"Oh sure! Bing . . . er . . . Andrew. You know Andrew?"

She moved slightly, with deliberate care, on the wobbly seat. "He was one of my pupils."

"You're a teacher?"

Disappointment showed on Clara's face. "Katie hasn't told you I teach second grade in Smithfield?"

"Katie hasn't told me much of anything," he said, gently.

She looked away, then, and sighed.

In the awkward silence that followed, she gazed around the tiny cluttered office, a gaze that took in the old sofa against one wall—springs showed through the sagging cushions—the cardboard boxes in one corner, the small table covered with papers, magazines and manuals that was being used as a desk, and a map tacked on a wall.

"She's quit talking altogether, now," Clara finally spoke. "I know she didn't talk much with other people. She did talk with me before . . ."

Watching closely, he saw her cheeks flush. "Before?"

Uncertain how to continue, she became more flustered and then angry with herself for losing her poise. Her chair creaked, warningly.

"You're not what I expected," she said at last.

"What were you expecting?" he asked, although he knew.

"Someone who was . . . ," she stammered. Her chair had begun making ominous sounds of protest as a result of her uncomfortable fidgeting.

"Younger?" he prompted, "more handsome—debonair, maybe?"

The alarmed expression on her face reflected the accuracy of his supposition. "No, no! That's not what I . . ."

"Steely-eyed? Silk-scarfed?" He went on, mercilessly. "Knee-booted? Leather-jacketed? Mustached?"

Watching him twist the ends of an imaginary mustache brought a chuckle from the woman. "Please!" She held up her hands as if to ward off further verbal assault.

"How about goggle-helmeted?" He was grinning at her.

"I give up!" She was beginning to relax. "I guess I asked for that."

He released a long, drawn out sigh. "All us aviators can't be Roscoe Turner, you know."

The chair, upon which he settled himself with practiced care, showed more than a passing resemblance to the one under Clara. "Now what was it you wanted to see Roscoe about?"

She smoothed the skirt across her lap and looked at the floor. "I wanted to find out what was going on." A chorus of squeaks and squeals emitted from the tortured frame beneath her until, alerted, she froze her position.

He pondered her statement and realized that the implication behind her words was not totally unexpected.

"Missus Stuart," he spoke each word separately and distinctly, "I've been teaching your daughter to fly an airplane and that's it."

Clara looked directly into his eyes. "Why?"

He matched her stare.

"For six-dollars an hour—that's why!"

"For money?" Her lips tightened. "She works like a dog—thinning beets, hoeing—and gives all that money to you." The chair was screaming with anguish. "I can't, for the life of me, imagine why she'd want to go up in one of those things."

The pilot was on his feet, glaring. "Missus Stuart, I didn't drag your daughter out of the beet field and throw her into my airplane. She came to me!"

He paced the small room, hands jammed in his pockets. "She didn't tell me where the money was coming from. I assumed she was getting it from her folks like the rest of the kids."

Clara's angry eyes followed him. "I can't afford to throw away good money for that sort of silliness. I'm only a teacher!"

"But what about your husband?" he asked, impatiently.

The sounds from her chair ceased abruptly. The fire that had flared about her moments before, faded. "Katie's father died when she was five," she said evenly.

He stared at the woman for a long moment. "Oh hell!" He sagged against the wall and held out his hands imploringly. "Forgive me. I didn't know."

He was silent, lost in thought for a time. "That could explain a lot," he said at last. "The stutter, I mean."

Clara nodded. "It started right after. Not much at first, but then it got worse—especially after we moved here."

He pushed away from the wall and sat down again. "You've tried to get her helped, I suppose?"

The woman's face registered disgust. "The doctor's around here say there's nothing wrong with her—physically—and that she might outgrow it in time. That's a lot of help."

He nodded, sadly. "What a shame. She's such a fine young lady—so bright and quick. Got the makings of a top-notch pilot, too."

Clara took a deep breath. "I've told her she has to stop."

He sat without moving. Be careful, he cautioned himself wondering what his next words should be. "That's your prerogative as a mother," he said finally. "I guess you've got your reasons."

Clara's eyes flashed. "She deceived me! I had no idea what she was doing! Mabel Bingstrom told me about it in church last Sunday. Can you imagine how I felt? She lied to me, her mother! She lied to me all this time!"

Torment showed on her face. He saw she was close to tears. "Missus Stuart," he began quietly, "I didn't know. I'm sure I must have asked if she had permission. I always do."

He leaned forward on his chair, seeking her eyes. "Missus Stuart, I'm a parent myself. I wouldn't want anyone messing in the lives of my kids and me not knowing about it."

He settled back on his chair and waited for her reaction. None came. She sat quietly, hands folded in her lap. Now he wondered why she remained in the little office, sitting on a tottery chair. Logically she should have stormed out after the first angry words, warning him never to see her daughter again.

Then he understood. She was troubled. She wanted to talk. "Katie must have wanted, very much, to do this thing," he suggested.

"She could have asked. We could have talked about it." Her chair had begun, once more, to voice its objections.

"And if she still wanted to fly?" he insisted.

Her look was hard—determined. "It's my responsibility to make decisions that are in her best interests."

"Of course," he agreed hurriedly. "How's she taking it?"

Her stare never wavered from his face for, what seemed, a long period and then he saw, to his great distress, the pools forming in her eyes.

"Oh Gosh!" He was on his feet, standing helplessly as she buried her face in her hands.

He continued hovering over her during the uncomfortable minutes that followed, murmuring sounds of sympathy while she dabbed her eyes and blew into a pathetically small handkerchief.

When, at last, she had some small control of herself, words poured out in a torrent. "She stays in her room. Hardly ever comes out. She doesn't even look at me when I go in. Acts like she's deaf when I'm talking to her. I've tried everything. She used to like going shopping in Logan, having lunch at the Bluebird, taking in a movie. Now she doesn't care about anything. It's been four days now. She won't eat. I've put food In her room. She won't touch it. I'm so worried."

The pilot experienced a moment of panic when it appeared she might start crying again, but with several deep breaths, she regained her composure.

"I couldn't imagine how she could be so upset about anything so silly. I thought it must be something else." Embarrassment showed on her face. "A boy."

He couldn't help but grin. "Mister Turner?"

She looked away, quickly.

"Her big love affair is with that Piper Cub out there," he said and then added, "the airplane," in answer to her questioning glance.

"But why?" Clara's expression was one of exasperation.

"I could make a guess, for what it's worth."

She nodded for him to continue.

"My hunch is that flying makes her feel . . . ," he groped for a word, . . ." unique—special."

"She's always been special to me."

He shook his head. "Of course. That's understandable. She's a very special girl, but it's not enough. She needs the attention of others—particularly those her own age—and, maybe more than that, she needs to feel important to herself."

Clara's look was skeptical. "And you think flying is doing that for her?"

He frowned, thinking. "Well, maybe you can answer that better than I can. Except for the last few days, have you noticed any difference in her over the past couple of months?"

He could almost read her thoughts by the changing expressions on her face. "She's been like a different person," Clara said finally. "Actually cheerful, like she hasn't been in years." She was staring out the window, wonderingly. "But it's so scary—so dangerous," she said, as if to herself.

Her gaze took in the scene outside—the blue sky beyond the trees with a trace of high cloud. A chicken hawk seemed suspended over the meadow for a long moment before swooping downward.

"How do you know that?" he asked, breaking into her thoughts so that she jerked her head around.

"Huh?"

"Have you ever been in an airplane?"

The chair creaked menacingly as she shifted her position. "Well . . . no, but . . ."

His good-natured grin masked the sarcasm behind his words. "How can an intelligent person like yourself make a judgment so final regarding something she knows absolutely nothing about? And as for danger," he said, pointing, "it's a damn sight safer than that chair you're sitting on."

* * *

Later that day when Clara, with elaborate casualness, sauntered into Katie's room and said, "Guess who I've been flying with?" she had her daughter's full and immediate attention.

Chapter 19

"Well I'll be goddamned! Katie! You look like somethin' the cat drug in." His words reverberated around the barnyard.

Bart was standing by the tractor, the crank held in one big hand, as the embarrassed girl approached. Duke barked a welcome and put a wet nose into her outstretched hand.

"You're ready for work, I see." He nodded at the lunch sack and the water jug she carried. "Your ma says you was sick." His face showed honest concern. You don't hafta if you don't feel up to it. Those spuds'll keep.

Her answer was a shy smile and a quick shake of the head. The big farmer grunted acknowledgment and turned to the tractor. He checked the gearshift lever, throttle and choke—his movements measured and deliberate.

Katie placed the sack and jug on the hay wagon that was hooked to the tractor and walked into the shed to fetch the hoe and file. When she returned, he was draining the gasoline sediment bowl. This done, he wiped his hands dry on the front of his bib coveralls and turned to the girl. "I ran into Alf Fletcher down at the pool hall Saturdee night. He told me somethin' that made me God-damn near drop m'cue stick."

He was studying her face as he talked. "Says his boy, Will, is flyin' one of them aeroplanes—says you was, too. Ever heerd anythin' so silly? Where you suppose he ever came up with an idee like that?

Katie grinned and ducked her head, blushing.

"Son of a bitch! So it's true!" he roared. "You never know with Alf. His line of bull shit stretches clear cross the valley. How come you never told me?"

The look on her face gave him the answer. "I see. Didn't tell your ma, neither, huh? Does she know, yet?"

Katie nodded.

"Bet she had a conniption."

This brought out a wry grin from the girl.

"But you're gonna keep doin' it?"

A bright smile accompanied the nod.

Excitement lit up the man's smooth, bronze face. "Hot damn! Now that's really somethin'! Whatever got you started?"

He didn't wait for an answer. His gaze had taken wings and was off somewhere over the girl's head, over the barn and over the summer clouds, that drifted like separate wads of white wool toward the eastern mountains. "Damn! You know, if I wasn't such an old fart . . ." The voice, which normally rattled the barn windows, had dropped to a whisper, carried away with his thoughts.

Duke bounded up onto the wagon and yelped for attention.

"Oh, so you're ready to go, are you? You noisy bastard." Bart rubbed the dog's muzzle with gloved hands.

If playing catch with the rubber ball was the black and white dog's first passion, then riding on the wagon had to qualify as second. On those occasion, when the wagon was loaded with pea vines, hay or straw, it became necessary for the husky farmer to heave the dog—all eighty pounds of him—on top of the load. There he would ride, king of the mountain, announcing his sovereignty with barking proclamations issued from his lofty perch.

Katie grasped the side rail and pulled herself up to sit on the edge of the wagon. She was unsuccessful in avoiding the slobbering tongue of the friendly animal.

Bart, shaking his head, started toward the tractor. Then he hesitated and turned back to Katie. "Is that the yeller one I been seein'?"

She nodded.

"Where do they keep the thing, anyway?"

She pointed southwest. "B . . . B . . . Benson."

Eyes wide, he bellowed, "Benson Ward? Well I'll be go to hell!" He lowered his voice. "Have you done it yourself. I mean without anybody helpin'?"

Her bright smile left no doubt.

"God!" he gasped. "Now ain't that somethin'! All by yourself." He regarded her tenderly. "I'm glad for you, girl. I'm glad you're doin' it. It's the right thing and I'm proud of you."

Katie swallowed the lump that came into her throat. The love was showing in his eyes.

"Hell!" he said, chuckling, "Only way I could be gladder is if you'd take me with you sometime. Have you took anybody before?"

She shook her head.

"Good! Let me be your first one."

'I . . . I will." she blurted out.

"Is that a promise?"

The girl nodded, solemnly.

"Okay. Let's get to work."

* * *

As if nothing had happened, Katie resumed flying. She'd missed four days of work so that all she had to give her instructor. The following Sunday, was two dollars and some odd change. This calculated into twenty-five minutes of solo flight. Usually she flew for an hour or more. Crow cheerfully told her to fly whatever she wanted—that he would put the difference on the cuff.

He never mentioned the visit by her mother and the self-conscious girl was grateful for that.

Her flights, over the next couple of weeks, took her meandering around the valley—seeing from above the familiar features of the area and orienting herself to this new perspective. She made numerous circuits of Smithfield. Over her home ground, she would retard and reapply engine power several times in succession—a signal to her mother and the Johnsons. To the young pilot, it seemed as if they were waiting in anticipation, for they would quickly appear in their respective yards to wave and watch the yellow airplane wag its wings in return.

On Sundays, following that period when she thought she would rather be dead, Katie flew in a state of high exhilaration. No longer was the black cloud of guilt hovering over her. Now her mother knew about her flying and, grudgingly, acquiesced.

Bart, of course, was ecstatic. His proud extolling of Katie's aeronautical capability sent those within earshot scurrying for cover.

Life continued, much as before, but she knew she could never be the same person after that day with Dwaine underneath the apple tree. She did, however, gain peace of mind and profound relief when her period occurred on schedule.

Katie's life, by her interpretation, was divided into two parts: Sunday when she flew and the rest of the week when she didn't fly. Most of those long, tedious hours of work, when not airborne, was spent daydreaming or reading about airplanes, aviators/aviatrixes, and flight. She read practically every book, on those subjects, that the Smithfield library stocked. Among those were: "Women And Flying" by Sophie Heath. "Girl Around The World"—Dorothy Kilgallen, George Hutchinson's "Flying Family" books, Bess Moyer's "Girl Flyer" series, "Solo Flight" by Jean Batten and a new book, just released, Faith Cuthreil's "The Heart Has Wings". As would be expected, she preferred those books written by women authors.

She carried a book with her, tucked into her trousers in the small of her back, as she hoed Bart's fields. Kept in this fashion, the book was readily available for her to quickly scan a page or two without much interruption of the work. Missus Albright, at the library, carefully ignored the dirt and sweat stains on the books returned by the shamefaced girl.

If she had tried to explain her infatuation with flying, Katie would have been unable to identify the reasons. Not that she didn't, at times, indulge in introspection. Perhaps more often than most people, she tried to analyze her feelings, but with something short of complete honesty. This stemmed from a reluctance to approach her innermost self too closely—the process was just too painful. She held herself accountable for her inability to deal with her stuttering problem and her self-respect suffered. The flip answer, "it's fun," that she gave Dwaine, when he asked why she flew, concealed a complex assortment of influences that compelled the young girl in this chosen undertaking.

One of these would be the challenge. Katie was gifted with an inquiring mind and an overwhelming desire for personal achievement. She had to try everything. Do everything. The tractor had been one such challenge.

Bart was one of the first, in the community, to own a tractor—an Allis-Chalmers. Early on he taught the youngster to steer the tractor, at a crawl, between rows of piled hay or pea vines while he loaded the attached wagon. When this routine began, it had been necessary for her to use both feet to depress the stiff clutch pedal. After she'd gained the size and strength to crank the engine, she operated the machine quite freely in the fields—sometimes on the back country roads. On two successive Saturdays, during the past spring planting season, she'd plowed the fields with the tractor while Bart followed with his team of horses pulling a harrow.

Katie also enjoyed driving automobiles. Compared with the tractor's noisy, jolting ride and coarse controls, her mother's Chevrolet and Bart's Plymouth sedan handled with quiet smoothness.

Here, again, was challenge but not so frequently experienced. There just seemed to be too few opportunities for her to practice.

Clara's own timid approach, to automobile operation, provided her daughter a reluctant and edgy instructor. Bart, on the other hand, seemed relaxed as he sat beside her—almost to the point of indifference—and that was nearly as distracting as her mother's nervousness.

The challenge was, no doubt, a contributing factor to Katie's interest in flying, but other elements may have been even more significant:

The pure sense or freedom—both physical and emotional—that piloting an airplane gave to the impressionable young woman, was a motivational force that could not be denied. In the sky, she felt as if she had control of her life. A movement of the stick or rudder bar took her on a course dictated only by impulse. Her constraints were the clock and her limited financial resources.

Back on the ground, it was a different matter. It seemed that almost every activity, in which she was involved, was governed by her mother, or Bart, or her teachers. And now, Crow. Not that she always resented their imposition—she hadn't yet reached that stage of maturity where she felt confident in her ability to conduct her own affairs without guidance.

Her mother had always been the dominant force in her life, allowing Katie to make only minor decisions for herself. The girl had been resigned, if not content, having her parent manage her affairs. It was easier that way. Obedience was deeply ingrained in her personality. Lately, however, she was beginning to assert herself in small ways. Although she dreaded the contention with her mother that these actions sometimes produced, she intuitively felt it was necessary if she were ever to become her own person.

Seeking out Bart's companionship had been a form of escape for the youngster. Bart encouraged her to be more self-expressive which helped build her confidence. If not for the big farmer's influence, it is questionable whether she would have gone searching for the yellow airplane in the first place.

And so, while she enjoyed the freedom that came from being aloft, it would be wrong to suggest that flying did not give Katie a sense of power—a smug feeling of superiority over non-flyers. Along with that was a certain vindictiveness toward those ground-bound individuals who had been her tormentors over the years. Never would she have admitted, even to herself, having such feelings.

Anticipation of high adventure certainly must be included among the reasons for the girl to be attracted to the idea of flight. The chance to experience, first hand, the thrills and excitement that were portrayed in the many books she'd read or in the movies she'd seen, had a strong appeal to the girl.

Finally, as Crow had suggested to her mother, Katie wanted to be noticed, in a positive way, by her peers. To be known, only, as "Stuttern' Stuart", had been devastating to her ego. Although she had been conditioned to be reticent by the fear of ridicule, she desperately wanted to be communicative—to be accepted by those whom she held in high regard. These were the special people in school that had Katie's admiration and respect. Typically they were the comely, the intelligent, the socially adept segment that surfaces in any population and she yearned to be one of them.

But Katie didn't give much consideration to questions of why she flew—she just flew. There was nothing she had ever done that gave her so much pleasure. At times she would simply float along in a state of bliss, rocking the plane from side to side. Once in a while she would practice some of the training exercises, as Crow advised, but the effort was half-hearted. Stalls and spins were uncomfortable, S-turns over a road were boring, takeoffs were needed only to get her into the sky and landings to bring her back to earth.

Then the day came when she had her first real scare.

It had been a glorious day—everything right. The morning air was so smooth it was like gliding through whipped cream.

On an impulse, she opened the split door, both the window and the bottom section, so that the whole right side was open to let in the sound and the feel of flight. She put her hand through the opening and wiggled her fingers in the air.

How wonderful it was to drift along, a few hundred feet above the ground, weaving, circling, looking at everything—cars on the road, folks milling about in front of the church, some children paddling a raft on a slough—a complete freedom. She was content to let each new attraction determine her route.

She laughed at a herd of sheep grazing on the hill-side. Little white piss-ants, she thought. It was exciting to fly alongside the western hills, a hundred yards away, following the contours. This game held her interest for some time and when she reluctantly turned away from the hill (which had, quite unexpectedly, become a mountain) her mind was slow to absorb the fact that she was looking out over totally unfamiliar terrain,

When it came, the knowledge caused her to flush and perspire in spite of the cool air whipping through the open door. Whimpering, she wrenched the airplane into turns, this way and that, hoping to see something recognizable. Everything was changed, as if she had stepped through the looking glass, like Alice, into another world.

The valley had undergone an amazing transformation into something entirely different. On the far side she could see only low, barren hills with stretches of empty plains—not the green carpet of fields that reached up toward the magnificent Wasatch Range.

Desperately she looked for a place to land, but it all looked so hostile—so foreign. There was an unfamiliar highway winding along the foot of the mountain and small rivers, none of which resembled the Bear River. Circling aimlessly, she tried to steel herself against rising panic. "Think!" she shouted to herself. "Th . . . think!"

The gas level indicator, in front of the windshield, caught her eye. Not much more than an inch of the rod was visible. The tank had been less than half full when she started out.

"Enough for an hour or so," Crow had told her.

"Think!" she told herself again, closing the door and window to subdue the nerve-shattering racket.

Then, in her mind, she heard Crow's words. "Climb! If ever you're lost, climb. You can't see anything crawling around in the weeds and bushes. Stand up tall!"

Without hesitation she jammed the throttle full forward and pulled on the stick.

"Please, M . . . Mister Piper," she prayed, using body movement to urge the airplane upward. "Please!"

Slowly the craft rose, bringing into view new hills, valleys and plains. From her elevated vantage point, Katie saw, what appeared to be, a huge body of water. Checking her compass, she decided it was south of her position. This only added to the confusion of the frightened girl. She knew of nothing like that in Cache Valley.

Could it be Bear Lake? she wondered trying to recall details of the map Crow had tacked to his office wall, but her mind refused to function.

Looking at the slowly descending mountain off the left wing, it occurred to her that she had never flown so high, not even for spin practice. The altimeter showed almost eight-thousand feet and still the mountain loomed above her. Cautiously she edged closer to its rocky outcroppings and felt the airplane surge upward in the rising air. Wind must be blowing into the mountain from my side and giving me an updraft, she realized, just like Crow said it would.

With the airplane soaring toward the top of the mountain's long ridge, she experienced a giddy feeling of excitement, of anticipation. And when she crested the ridge, another valley had come into view—a beautiful, green valley with a grand wall of mountains on the opposite side.

Then she saw it, Ol' Flat Top, and she shrieked with joy and relief.

The full comprehension of her folly came quickly. What a dumb shithead! she cursed herself. I've been out in the Salt Lake Valley! I flew right around Wellsville Mountain!

Of course Crow had known. "Got lost, huh?" he asked as she climbed out of the Cub, shaken and embarrassed.

He always knows. Katie remembered. He hadn't scolded her, but he had been strangely quiet afterwards.

Chapter 20

Katie was angry and disappointed. No one had mentioned her. Hell! I'm a pilot, too! she wanted to scream. I'm not invisible, just because I'm a girl. Nevertheless, she was being ignored by the other student pilots.

She stood silent, brooding, listening to plans being made for the contest. The animated chatter washed over her in waves: ". . . put up posters in the store windows, . . . know where I can borrow a public-address system, . . . signs on the highway at the Loganna turnoff, . . . flags, . . . notices in the Herald Journal newspaper and announcements broadcast by KVNU radio, . . . banners."

It had all started with a flat tire on the Cub. When Katie arrived, she found the instructor inside the building, wrestling with the problem of getting the wheel off the airplane as it sat with one wing drooping sadly over the squashed tire.

"Help me with this," he directed. "I left my jack at home. When I push up on the wing struts, put those blocks under the axle."

He grasped the two struts adjacent to the wing attachments and pushed upward with a grunt. With the wing tilted and the little wheel lifted off the ground. Katie quickly positioned the blocks.

"Must've picked up a nail," he gasped, releasing his hold. "Could damned easily have happened in here."

She handed him the tools as he worked to remove and disassemble the wheel. It had been a nail and he cursed himself for being so careless during construction of the building.

"We'll have to wait for Dwaine," he announced. "I don't have any tire patches, either."

The first thought that came into the young woman's mind was to leave immediately to avoid seeing him. No!

she told herself, firmly. I'm not going to run like a scared little rabbit and miss out on the flying.

This self-inflicted admonition failed to defeat her nervousness and when Dwaine walked in, with a barely perceptible nod of greeting, they eyed each other warily.

"Tell 'im, Crow." the inevitable Will followed his friend inside, causing Katie to groan, inwardly. "Tell 'im that a license does not a pilot make. Even if the examiner is crazy enough to fly with 'im and even if dumb luck gets 'im past the checkride, he won't be one bit better than he is right now."

This light-hearted altercation, between the two had, obviously, been going on for some time.

"Don't get me involved in this," the instructor told them.

"You have to understand," Dwaine patiently explained to his partner, "a pilot's license is like a badge of merit that distinguishes the superb flyer, like myself, from the crappy ones, like you."

"Crappy! Crappy!" Will's voice rose to new heights. "That does it! You show me your best stuff today, I'm gonna beat it!"

"Not in my airplane you don't!" The instructor's voice held an edge in spite of the grin on his lined face.

"Aw come on, Crow!" the big youth protested. "You heard 'im dishonor the proud name of Fletcher. Why my granddaddy just rolled over in his grave. I can't let 'im get away with that. How can I prove to Smilin' Jack here, who's the best pilot?"

"By living longer," the instructor answered instantly.

The friendly argument raged back and forth while the tire was being repaired and installed. By then, Tweet Anderson arrived and actively engaged in the discussion. "How you goin' to let this pair decide who's top dog around here, anyway?" he asked the older man.

Crow considered the question for a moment before answering. "Why don't you each make three landings out there today and I'll be the judge of who does the best."

"That's only one part of flying," the blond young man disagreed. "They've got to do more than that."

The instructor shrugged. "Could be. Give me a hand here."

The youths assisted in moving the airplane out of the building, onto the grass and into the sunlight. With Katie at the controls, the craft soon departed leaving the turmoil behind.

Off the ground, she immediately forgot the discussion and gave her attention over to the beautiful day, the airplane and the flight.

The air was remarkably quiet. Katie was no longer as concerned with turbulence in the air as she had been when she started flying. Still, on this morning as at any other time, Katie appreciated the air being smooth.

With the Cub floating along at reduced power a few hundred feet above the ground, she enjoyed the view and the sense of solitude.

Bart had told her, the day before, that he would be out at the leased pasture checking on a heifer that was due to freshen.

Katie headed the plane in that general direction, hoping that he would still be there. She spotted his Plymouth parked in the lane and then saw the farmer standing near the five head of stock in the field. From her low altitude she recognized Peaches, a three-year old Holstein, from the cow's unusual markings—mostly black on both ends and white in the middle.

Katie had named the heifer, when she had seen it as a yearling, nibbling on the ripe fruit that had dropped to the ground in the little orchard near the house.

Peaches had not yet given birth—there was no calf to be seen from the airplane as it circled above the pasture. The pilot laughed, seeing the big man cavorting and waving.

Watching the activity below, Katie almost failed to notice the hazardous situation that was developing. Her first sense of awareness came from her buttocks, as Crow had predicted.

Listen to your 'butt'," he had told her. If your butt doesn't feel right, something's haywire. It's known as 'flying by the seat of your pants'."

Warned by the increased pressure in her seat, she looked forward and saw the valley tipped near vertical in the windshield. By this time the control stick had begun the familiar shake that signaled a stall—in this case, a high-speed stall.

Katie reacted instantly, applying full throttle and releasing the backpressure that had been pulling the airplane into an increasingly tight circle. With stick and rudder bar, she rolled the wings level, allowing a loss of altitude in order to regain airspeed. Less than a hundred feet separated the craft from the pasture grass before full control was reestablished.

White-faced and trembling, the young pilot turned and began climbing on a southerly heading that would take her back to the airstrip.

I'm sure glad Bart didn't know what was going on back there. Katie felt some relief at the thought. He would've shit his britches if he'd known how close I came to dumping this Cub in his lap.

"What a d ... dumb trick to p ... pull!" the girl yelled at herself in the stifling enclosure. "And after Crow had w ... war ... warned what could happen!"

God! Katie reflected. It's a good thing my butt was talking to me.

By the time she returned, more members had been added to the group—Bing and Bob. She quickly forgot her near mishap upon learning of the contest being planned—a big contest to coincide with the Cache County Fair that could be attended by families, friends and the public. Intrigued, Katie stayed to listen to the excited discussion of events and rules, accompanied by hand demonstrations and diagrams drawn in the dirt. Each of the young men had taken on specific assignments for the many preparation tasks. Though she waited, expectantly, on the fringe of the group, no one acknowledged her presence or invited her participation.

In turn, individuals left the gathering to fly the Cub but their absences were abnormally brief. Each returned with new ideas, for the event, to be considered.

Katie tarried until the sun began dipping toward the western hills and she could feel her stomach protesting a lack of nourishment. Her anger changed to sad disillusionment at being overlooked. She continued to linger, however, as the arrangements were finalized and the group began to disband with shouts of: "God! Look at the time!" and, "My ol' man's gonna kick my ass!"

Then in a melee of roaring auto engines, spinning tires, honking and yelling, they were gone.

Crow was in the office making notes on a scrap of paper as she approached and stood waiting.

He looked up, surprised to find her there. "Katie?"

She shifted from one foot to the other, but her look was direct. "M . . . m . . . me t . . . too."

"Huh?" He frowned, momentarily before comprehension came. "Oh, I see." He studied her face. "You don't really want to get into this, do you?"

She nodded.

"I'm sorry," he said. "It never occurred to me you'd be interested." He indicated his notes. "Do you have any idea what this is all about?"

After a moment's hesitation, she shrugged.

"Spot landings and even ribbon catching aren't so bad, but paper cutting takes some pretty fancy maneuvering. It's not exactly stunt-flying, which isn't your cup of tea if I remember correctly, but it does require some rather aggressive airplane handling."

Katie wilted visibly at the thought of spins and loops.

"It would take practice," he said gently, "disciplined practice and, from what I've seen lately, you haven't been putting much effort into improving your flying skills."

Tightened jaw muscles and a slight frown were the only outward indications of the resentment that was building in the girl.

"I don't know what you've been doing in the way of air-work, but your landings don't impress me much. What you did out there today looked pretty sloppy."

The hurt showed clearly in her eyes. Still, the instructor decided, it had to be said.

"It's my impression that your interest in flying is just joy riding, like last Sunday, and that bothers me. I've got too much invested in that piece of equipment to want it in the hands of a half-trained pilot."

His reference to the previous Sunday when she'd become lost and remembering the close call she'd experienced a short time ago, caused the girl to blush furiously. The shame she felt was so obviously displayed that he was instantly sorry.

"Katie," he said softly, "I know how well you can fly when you put your mind to it. I want you to fly because it means so much to you. But I want you to be a good pilot and I want you to be a safe pilot.

"I don't think you could be ready for the contest. It's only a few weeks away. You probably wouldn't have time even if you flew more than just a couple of times on Sunday."

The serious eyes, that met his, held so much sorrow that he felt himself yielding. "Of course there's some techniques that would be useful but, mostly, it's a matter of just going out and practicing."

"W . . . woo . . . w . . . would you . . . hel . . . hel . . . p?" Her gaze wavered.

His heart went out to her, realizing what it must have cost her to speak those few words, but he couldn't let her know. Not yet.

"You mean special instruction?" He looked at her steadily.

She shrugged, slightly, averting her eyes.

"You want me to give you preferential treatment?"

Katie found something on the floor that needed all her attention.

"Being female doesn't automatically bestow upon you inalienable privileges in the aeronautics world."

He'd begun using his "four dollar words", but she wasn't quite certain he was teasing.

"Do you honestly believe I would compromise my integrity so that you could exercise an unscrupulous supremacy over that collection of plebeians?"

She was watching his face from under her brows— the corners of her mouth twitched upward.

"How could you have acquired the impression, over our rather brief acquaintance, that I was so completely devoid of character?"

Her smile was in full bloom and he let the last of his implied resolve disintegrate. "Well, what the hell!" He heaved a long, mock sigh. "Still got a little daylight left. We may as well get started."

Chapter 21

"Ladies and gentlemen." Crow spoke experimentally into the microphone. "You folks hear me alright out there?"

He sighted a few nods at the edge of the crowd and was satisfied. Must be over five-hundred people here, he thought, wonderingly.

Crow really hadn't expected many more than just the families and friends of his students, but there they were, adults and children—most wearing their Sunday best—standing in clusters or sitting on blankets spread on the grass. Bob's sisters had asked if they could set up a stand under the trees to sell lemonade and hot dogs. Already they were doing a brisk business.

"We want to thank you for coming out today." He gained confidence from the smiles around him and went on. "These young pilots should put on quite a show for you."

His extended arm brought attention to the six contestants standing in a row to his right. "Let me introduce you to the pilots. They'll step forward as I call their names. First, Scott Anderson, known as Tweet."

The blond youth, at the head of the line, stepped out of the rank and raised his hand bashfully.

"Scott is eighteen, lives in Hyrum and graduated from South Cache High. He plans to start at the Agricultural College this fall. Let's wish him luck."

There was a smattering of applause, mostly from a blond middle age couple with two towheaded young boys.

"By the way, folks, you'll be meeting the pilots in the same order they'll be competing. We had a drawing earlier today to set it up."

Crow looked over at Dorothy, sitting with their sons. She smiled encouragement.

"Next I'd like you to meet Willard Fletcher. Will graduated from North Cache this year. He just turned nineteen. Happy birthday, Will."

The big youth grinned, shaking his head with good humor. "That wuz last week and I didn't git no present from you."

Crow laughed, a sound that roared through the loudspeakers. "Maybe you'll get it today, but you'll hafta win it."

Katie was starting with a bad case of the jitters, which she knew would become worse the longer she waited. Just my luck to be the last one, she thought, but I've got to stop worrying about that.

Standing next to Dwaine did little to relieve her anxiety. When she closed her eyes, she could still feel his presence. I hate him, she reminded herself, . . . I think.

A sudden thought grabbed her. I wonder if any of these people here know about me and Dwaine? Cautiously she looked at their faces. Whether they were sneering at her or merely squinting in the bright sun, she could not be certain.

God! What if they know!

She risked a glance at the young man next to her. You son of a bitch! she screamed soundlessly. If you told Will, you probably blabbed to everyone else in Cache Valley.

She longed to sit down on the blanket with her mother before her legs failed her completely. Clara smiled, reassuringly, at her daughter from under a broad-brimmed hat.

Katie heard Dwaine's name booming from the loudspeakers. Oh God! she almost spoke aloud. I'm next! What should I do? Wave? Bow?

Then it was her name. Somehow she managed to step up beside Dwaine and raise her hand timidly. She was barely aware of Crow's words, ". . . seventeen, . . . Smithfield, . . . North Cache High . . ." She tried to smile, but found she couldn't. Her face muscles refused to function.

Finally it was over and she was, miraculously, still standing, although weak and nauseous.

Crow grinned with satisfaction at the crowd's reaction to Katie.

"Look! One of 'em's a girl!'"

"Is she gonna fly?"

The children pushed close, staring up into the tall girl's face—unbelieving. "Wow!"

Katie expelled a gasp of relief when he finally made the announcement. "Okay Tweet? Dwaine, will you pull the prop for him? The rest of you can take it easy."

As Katie collapsed, gratefully, beside her mother, Crow's voice continued to penetrate the soporific atmosphere that prevailed on the soft, summer day.

"The contest is made up of three parts that involve precision flying, maneuvering and good judgment. These are paper cutting, ribbon pickups and spot landings. Now I'll describe each of these events as we go along."

He paused to look around, the grin on his lined face showing his enjoyment. "Each pilot," he continued, "will fly for twenty to twenty-five minutes. He . . . or she . . . ," Katie caught his wink, ". . . will perform all three events in sequence."

"First the paper cutting. Now these pilots have been practicing for the last couple of weeks. During this period, their mothers may have wondered why all the toilet paper was disappearing."

There was an appreciative chuckling from the crowd.

'Well I can clear up that mystery right now . . . did you say something, Will?"

The youth stepped up and spoke directly into the microphone. "I said we don't got a single Sears or Wards catalog left."

The shrill squeals from the ladies, mingling with the men's guffaws, answered Will's outburst as he was playfully shoved away from the microphone.

"As I was saying," Crow began once more, "if you've been missing rolls of toilet paper, that may have been it you saw drifting down from the sky the past couple of weekends."

As the laughter continued, he turned and winked at his wife.

"Now when you drop a roll of toilet paper out of an airplane, it unrolls to form a streamer about a hundred feet long. These pilots will use the airplane propeller, like a big pair of scissors, to cut this paper as it falls. I'll describe the ribbon pick and spot landing events a little later.

"Each pilot will perform each of the three events three times. A maximum of one-thousand points can be earned, three-hundred for each event, plus one-hundred points which is granted if he . . ." Katie's face reddened once more as his nod directed the crowd's attention to her. ". . . or she follows the rules of safe aircraft operation."

The clatter of the yellow airplane's engine startup interrupted the speaker's recital and brought excited yells from the children. Dwaine stepped off to the side and waved to the pilot. The propeller became a blurred circle and the sound level changed as the craft began to move awkwardly down the strip—little doughnut tires seeking and finding irregularities in the grassy surface.

Dwaine shooed back to the congregation, several over-eager youngsters, who had ducked under the rope barricade.

"Please, folks!" Crow implored, "Keep your children away from the area where the airplane will be operating. We don't want any accidents to spoil this grand day."

Emphasis was given his words by a raw-boned man, dressed in bib overalls. Who grabbed one of the scalawags and gave him a pop to the back of the head.

Crow hastened to drown out the boy's yell with the loudspeaker. "For this first event, Tweet . . . er . . . Scott, that is Scott Anderson, will climb to fifteen-hundred feet above the ground. He has with him three rolls of toilet paper. When he's directly out in front of us, he will throw one roll out of the airplane. Those of you with field glasses should be able to see the paper after it unravels. I'll be watching," he held up a pair of binoculars, "so the rest of you folks will have to take my word for it."

Katie sat beside her mother, shivering with apprehension. She heard the Cub's roar. Checking the mags, she realized. Oh my God! I won't remember a thing.

But then her mother took hold of her hand and it helped—a little.

"After he's thrown out the paper," Crow continued, "Scott will turn back and try to cut the paper with the plane's propeller. Now then . . . ," his voice took on a confidential note, ". . . it's necessary that Scott make his turns correctly. Otherwise he may not see the paper at all because the wing blocks his vision in a turn."

At the sound of the engine's tempo increasing, all heads turned as one to watch the bright yellow airplane on its takeoff run. The craft skipped lightly off the higher protrusions on the field as it passed the crowd, then lifted and climbed into the cloudless sky. Spontaneous applause broke out among the observers.

"Ain't it pretty, though!" Crow could not conceal his pride and the people laughed their appreciation.

"It'll take him about five minutes to reach his altitude," the cheerful announcer went on. "He will attempt to cut each streamer twice. Each time he's successful is worth fifty points. Two rules apply here—he must not lose control of the airplane and he must stay between one-thousand and fifteen-hundred feet above the ground during these maneuvers. This doesn't allow him much time to make two passes, so he can't let any grass grow under his feet."

While the spectators pivoted in place, watching as the airplane circled the field gaining altitude, Crow kept a running commentary, describing each action the pilot was performing—trying to make his listeners part of the activity occurring inside the airplane. And they stood there, with hats or hands shading their eyes, watching and listening intently.

Katie's stomach was churning. She was on her feet with the rest, gazing upward—hoping that Tweet did good. She hoped they all did good and not embarrass themselves in front of the viewers. Katie wanted the people entertained, since they were mostly poor farm folk who had little to brighten their drab lives. At this moment their spirits were soaring upwards with the yellow airplane.

The narration, being emitted from the public-address system, broke into her thoughts.

"The gentlemen out on the field are Lowell Jorgensen and Rolf Simonds."

The two grinned, bashfully, at the audience.

"They're setting up the poles for the ribbon pickup event."

Several members of the crowd took notice. "Hey Rolf!" one shouted, "Somebody finally got you to do some work."

"More'n they'd git from you," came the laughing reply.

"Take it easy on 'em." Crow interjected. "They're gonna' put in a long day, hanging ribbons and checking spot landings. I haven't told 'em, yet. There's no pay."

"Hear that, Rolf?" the same voice bawled. "No pay! Maybe you can get one of the pilots to make a donation to trade for a little help."

The younger man on the field faced his heckler, hat thrown back—grinning widely. "That's the ticket!" he yelled. "Send over that lil' gal. We might be able to work somethin' out."

A chorus of laughter enveloped Katie, who turned away quickly, face beet-red, and dropped down next to her mother.

Clara couldn't help but be amused by her daughter's prissiness. "Don't let them get your goat, honey." she said, striving vainly to conceal a smile. "They just like to tease."

The loudspeakers blared again. "Okay, folks! It looks like Scott has the altitude and is lining up for his first run."

Crow was holding the binoculars to his eyes with one hand while gripping the microphone with the other. All heads were turned upward. A few binoculars were being passed around frantically amid cries of, "Lemme see! Lemme see!"

The engine sound changed to a quieter level.

"There goes the first roll of paper!"

"Ooooooo's" and "aaaaah's" greeted the announcement. Most of the observers—those lacking binoculars—thought they were seeing the white streamer, even if they weren't.

"Now he's turning!" Crow's voice crackled in the air. Maybe he didn't turn far enough. Yup! He missed it!"

Groans of disappointment came from the crowd.

"He's turning back! Turning! Turning! He's straightening up. It's gonna be close! He's got it!"

His yell caused those near the loudspeakers to turn away, covering their ears. Dorothy rose from the blanket and hurried to her husband's side. He nodded, with a silly grin, as she whispered in his ear and pointed at the microphone.

"Now, folks," his voice was somewhat subdued, "he's climbing back to fifteen-hundred feet again. So far he has fifty points." Crow glanced at his wife who was writing in a small, blue notebook.

Katie had heard the airplane resume climbing and, shortly afterward, saw it straighten on a northerly heading.

"There it goes!" she heard him say and strained to catch sight of the second streamer.

"Not turning enough this time, either," she thought.

The announcer's voice confirmed her deduction. "He didn't see it."

She could see the airplane turning abruptly, straighten and then wander aimlessly about.

"He's lost it." Crow's voice sounded disappointed.

The roar of the engine told her that Tweet had given up and was going after his third try.

Excited yelps and pointed fingers brought attention to the separated sections of the first streamer coming in to view.

"Hope those cows make good use of all that paper."

Katie recognized Will's voice and his girl-like giggle over the laughter of others.

"Be a lot more sanitary if they did. Hee, hee, hee!"

She cursed him silently, Silly shithead! Then turned her eyes upward to watch Tweet's final attempt.

"Doing better this time, folks," the speaker assured them. "He's turned more. There! Right through the top!"

The loudspeakers whistled, protestingly. Crow's anxious glance found his wife holding a finger to her lips in a shushing gesture. He winked at her and looked to see the airplane turn again.

"Oh oh! Looks like he couldn't find it for the second cut. Think he flew right over it. That makes it one-hundred points."

The sound of the engine faded away which brought a little cry from the blond lady with the two small boys.

"It's alright. folks," he said quickly into the microphone to soothe the concerned mother. "He's just gliding down to do the ribbon pickup."

With that, he launched into a description of the event: "The plane has to be flown at just the correct height to catch the ribbon on the landing gear—the wheels. Too low and the propeller will cut the ribbon. Too high and he'll miss. If he catches it too far off center, the wind may pull it off the wheel struts."

Crow paused to look around for their nods of comprehension.

"Remember, he's got to fly away, with the ribbon trailing, to earn his hundred points. If the wheels touch the ground, that run is disqualified. He has three attempts."

Soon the putt-putt-putt of the idling engine and the whistling, rushing sounds of air could be heard as the aircraft turned to fly parallel with the field—descending. Periodically a brief roar of the engine could be heard.

"He'll make his approach from the south," the announcer told his audience, "so he'll pass in front of us from right to left."

He looked to make sure the two men were safely off to the side of the field.

The yellow airplane had slowed going away and, as it turned back toward the field, it appeared for a moment to be hanging still. But then it grew in size and soon the idling engine could be heard again.

"Here he comes, folks!"

The onlookers had formed a solid line abreast the rope barrier. Katie had managed to be in front.

Too high, she realized, and too fast!

Crow echoed her thoughts. "He may not be low enough to catch . . ."

His words were lost to the engine's roar as the airplane flashed over the brightly colored ribbon causing it to flutter wildly.

"Oh my!" The loudspeakers expressed the crowd's disappointment. "He missed by about six feet, but he still has two more chances to catch a ribbon and earn the hundred points each time."

The craft was climbing again, turning to the left.

"One thing I should tell you, folks. None of the pilots have had any practice for this event. They're all starting even."

Unnoticed by most of his listeners, the announcer took out a handkerchief and dried his forehead and hands . . . and I hope to God they're careful! he prayed silently.

That morning he had gathered the participants for a lecture that he counted on their remembering.

"With the excitement of a contest, the desire to win and all, there's a tendency for people to get carried away and do dumb things," he had told them. "Now the prizes aren't worth a busted head or a busted airplane, and I'm sure there's no one here who's pride can't stand not being the winner—or even coming in last."

He'd given Katie a hard look that made her squirm.

"I'm reserving the right to pull some or all of those one-hundred points if I see anything that looks like dangerous or sloppy piloting. I'll go further than that—I'll disqualify you from a run or the whole event if you do something really stupid."

He had been gratified that no one had joked or made light of his remarks. Even Will had remained serious.

"Now let's look at each event in turn," he had continued. "First, the paper cutting. You may try to make turns too tight, in getting back to the streamer, so you won't lose it. That isn't necessary—you've got plenty of time. If you get too reckless, you're going to get a high-speed stall. That yellow kite is going to try flipping over on its back and you'd better react pretty fast in getting things under control—you may have less than a thousand feet of altitude left and you'll need most of it to recover. If that happens, you might as well come back and land because I'm taking you out of the contest. So keep in mind, when you feel your butt pushing on the seat and the control stick pressure building up in a turn, ease off! You might be saving your life.

"In the ribbon pickup event, you only have to remember one thing: look straight ahead during your run. If you look down to see if you've caught the ribbon, there's a good chance you could fly right into the ground. That's why I objected to the flour bombing event. I've heard of guys that were so preoccupied with dropping the bomb that they forgot to fly the airplane. So watch that ribbon only through the windshield. You can check the landing gear for the ribbon while you're climbing back to pattern altitude. If you didn't catch the ribbon, you can check while you're flying your downwind leg to see if Lowell and Rolf are putting up a new one. If they are, that means you probably cut the last one with the prop and you can adjust your next pass accordingly.

"The ribbon will be about fifteen feet up, so your wheels shouldn't touch the ground, even if you were to fly under it. My advice is to fly right at the ribbon, level with the runway at reduced power—say eighteen-hundred revs—like you're making a wheel landing. Pull up a little just before you get to the ribbon, then full power and climb on out.

"Finally I want to say something about spot landings. Lowell and Rolf have been told to measure from the spot where the tail wheel is down to stay, with the main wheels planted on the grass, so it won't do any good to try forcing the plane down. It will just bounce off and make another landing further down the strip. And that's where it will be measured.

"Now, just one last thing. These are tests of good technique and good judgment. I can tell you right now, the erratic pilot doesn't stand a chance. This contest will be won by the person that demonstrates smooth, precision flying. I want to see everybody do their best out here today, so don't pull any boners and spoil the works for everyone."

Crow gripped the microphone with a white-knuckled hand as the airplane turned toward the grass strip. "This is Scott Anderson making his second attempt to catch the ribbon. Let's see how he does. Could be a little high again."

As he talked, he tried to will the airplane lower but to no avail. The bright orange ribbon remained suspended between the two bamboo poles as the craft climbed away.

"He's getting closer, folks, but he's being careful. He doesn't want to touch the ground." Crow realized, with a sense of relief, that at least one of his pilots had taken his message to heart.

"He's got one more chance to get a ribbon. After that he goes directly into the spot landing event . . . say now! I can use that . . . oops!"

Several-hundred astonished eyes were turned on the announcer, who was grinning with embarrassment as one hand covered the microphone. Dorothy was shaking with laughter as she held out a glass of lemonade to her husband.

"Excuse me," he mumbled an apology to his audience. Taking the glass, he drank deeply—gratefully. "Lifesaver," he whispered. kissing her on the cheek.

"Now then!" he said, smiling at those around him. This brought on a burst of laughter. "I want to give you a little background information regarding this next event. Some of you folks may have heard that an airplane will fall like a sack of cement if the engine ever stops. Nonsense! The plane will come down, of course, but slowly—gliding at fifty to sixty miles an hour."

He noted, with satisfaction, that he had their attention. "These aircraft engines are very reliable. It's unlikely that one will ever quit unless it runs out of gas. But pilots have to be trained to handle this situation, should it ever occur. They can't just pull over to the side of the road. That's why they get a lot of instruction and a lot of practice making spot landings.

"'Spot landing' means putting the aircraft down as close to a particular spot as possible. If ever it became necessary to make a landing in a pasture, where there wasn't much room, the pilot would want to touch down as near to one end of the field as possible, in order to get stopped before reaching the other end. If the airplane landed too soon or too late, it would probably tear up somebody's barbed wire fences and let loose a bunch of livestock. That could be real dangerous for a pilot having somebody coming after him with a pitchfork."

The crowd laughed easily along with the crinkle-faced man holding the microphone.

"To hit close to a particular spot, a pilot needs good judgment and correct planning so that the airplane is at the proper landing speed and height when he arrives at the spot."

Crow's discourse was interrupted by the sound of the engine as the yellow craft swept down toward the grass strip.

"Here we go!" the loudspeakers blared. "It's now or never! Looks low enough—he may get it!"

The airplane roared past, just clearing the grass until the last moment before reaching the ribbon, where it angled upward abruptly and began rising. The ribbon drifted to the ground in two pieces. "Oh, too bad!"

The narrator's outburst coincided with moans and groans from the spectators.

"I thought he had it that time, but he was a little low and cut it with the propeller."

As the airplane climbed and turned, one of the two men, standing off to the side of the strip, shouted a question.

"That's right, Lowell," Crow spoke into the microphone. "You can take down the poles now and get ready for spot landings."

As the poles were being pulled from sockets set in the turf, the now familiar voice of the announcer carried out over the green countryside.

"You folks may not be able to see it from here, but there's a wide calcimine powder line across the landing strip down toward the south end. Then, every ten yards this way from that location, there's a narrow line. The last one, out here in front of us, is one-hundred yards away from the wide line—that's the length of a football field.

"Now the object of this event is to land as close to the wide line—or 'spot'—as possible, but it must be on this side. A landing on the other side of the spot line will be disqualified. Lowell will be stationed down near the thirty-yard line. Rolf will be close to the eighty-yard line. They'll measure from where the airplane tail wheel touches and stays on the ground to the hundred-yard line. Right on the spot will count for one-hundred points. On the hundred-yard line and beyond is zero points. Halfway between is fifty points and so forth."

Crow looked at the faces nearby. "Did I make that clear?" He waited for a response.

A few nods provided the answer, so he gave his attention to the approaching airplane.

"Here he comes, ladies and gentlemen, Scott Anderson on his first spot landing attempt."

A brief burst of noise came from the engine as the craft aligned itself with the strip. Crow raised his binoculars as it came over the fence at the end of the field.

"Looks like he's gonna have a good one . . . there! That should be worth sixty or seventy points."

The airplane was on the ground—little wheels spinning vigorously as it crossed in front of the gaping crowd.

Then, with engine roaring, the tail lifted and the yellow craft was off and climbing.

The man, known as Lowell, lifted and lowered his right arm a total of six times—his left arm, twice.

"Sixty-two points for Scott. That gives him one-hundred sixty-two points, so far." He looked at his wife for affirmation. She nodded and wrote in the book.

Clara returned to her blanket on the grass, convinced it would be a long afternoon. She beckoned her daughter to join her. "You'd better take it easy, honey. You're going to be worn to a frazzle." She studied the young woman—flesh of her flesh—and saw the lines of anxiety on her face. How brown was the skin that showed.

If it wasn't for the hair, you'd think she was an Indian, Clara mused, and so thin—all that hard work in the sun.

She sighed, a mother concerned. Opening her purse, she handed over a dollar coin.

"Why don't you get some hot-dogs and lemonade for us. You haven't eaten since breakfast and not much then."

Katie put her hand to her stomach, made a face and shook her head.

"Honey," Clara pleaded, "you've got to stop fretting and take care of yourself or you're going to be in no condition to fly that airplane."

"The young girl looked at her mother and saw the concern. Finally, with a sigh, she took the money and rose. "See if they've got some catsup," Clara called.

Katie was diverted from her mission by the announcement of Scott's second landing. She quickly joined the line of observers and saw Rolf signal thirty-seven points after the airplane had become airborne once again.

"One-hundred and ninety-nine points for Scott," the crowd was told. "He has a possibility of making two-hundred and ninety-nine points if his final landing is perfect. He'll also get the extra hundred points if his piloting performance holds up. Whether that will be good enough to win some prizes, or not, well have to wait and see."

As the Cub lifted upwards under the midday sun, Crow looked at his watch. Thirty-two minutes he's been at it. Not too bad, he told himself. Let a couple more fly before I refuel.

"Oh yes, folks," he spoke into the microphone. "We do have prizes. For the first place winner, there will be three hours of free flight time worth fifteen dollars. Second place will be two hours and third place—one. The Bluebird cafe will set up a free meal for two, with all the trimmings, for the pilot who comes in first. Andersons has donated three dollars worth of merchandise for first place, two for second, one for third. Auerbachs is giving a fine wristwatch to the winner,

He continued naming prizes as the airplane turned toward the field. Local merchants had been more interested in the contest than was expected and surprisingly generous with their donations.

"Scott's been making some good landings in practice," he confided. "Let's see how he does on his last try. It could be close!"

The airplane touched the grass just beyond the spot line but then, to Crow's chagrin, bounced several feet upwards, hung momentarily and dropped firmly to the grass further down the strip.

The announcer's groan was audible through the public-address system as Rolf signaled twenty-three.

"Scott's final score is three-hundred and twenty-two points." This he confirmed with Dorothy while the airplane waddled back through the grass to the parking area. "Let's give Scott Anderson a big hand for a fine effort," Crow said as the Piper rolled to a stop.

The youth climbed from the airplane looking drawn and disappointed. He brightened, however, with the generous outburst of applause and strutted into the congregation to join his family.

Will Fletcher was announced as the next contestant. Laughing and joking, he made his way to the airplane. Shortly afterwards, the onlookers watched him depart, then settled themselves to watch the overhead performance. Many turned their attention to the refreshment stand where the Garrett sisters looked at each other, wondering if their supplies would be adequate.

Children were soon grouped and engaged in playing Tag and Ready Fox—running and yelling. Two elderly gentlemen moved over into the stand of trees alongside the road. There on the shaded grass they stretched out and, with hats covering their faces, promptly went to sleep. One stirred, briefly, sometime later when Will's girlish giggle was heard over the loudspeakers.

"Somebody up there is stealin' toilet paper," his bray could be easily distinguished. "I throw'd out three rolls and that's the last I ever saw of 'em."

As the repetitive activities continued into the afternoon, the atmosphere changed from excitement to one of languor. Each succeeding competitor had a decreasing number of observers come to the barricade to watch his ribbon pickup and spot landing attempts. Many were content to monitor the contest through Crow's announcements and commentary. Some had lost interest altogether. Groups sat chatting, satisfied for the occasion to visit with friends and relatives. Youngsters lay asleep on the blankets or in their mother's arms. An occasional young man and young woman paired off away from the others.

Picnic baskets had appeared and their contents consumed. People departed and others arrived to take their place.

The warm sun, the monotonous drone of the aircraft engine, coupled with the steady stream of words pouring from the loudspeakers, had a soothing, calming effect. With her hunger satisfied (at her mother's insistence) by another hot dog, Katie succumbed. Curled on the blanket, head on her mother's lap, she felt the tension leave her body. And then she slept.

Chapter 22

It was her mother's hand stroking her hair that brought her back to consciousness.

"Honey! Are you alright?"

She sat up, groggily—found her mother's anxious eyes.

"Are you sure you'll be able to fly?" Clara was saying. "You're so tired."

Katie brushed back the damp hair from her face and looked around, confused.

Crow's voice reached her. "That was a good one—worth eighty-three points. That gives Dwaine a grand total of five-hundred and seventy-seven points, which means he's beat out Bob Garrett to take the lead."

Katie tried to make sense out of the announcement. She caught a glimpse, between people, of the yellow airplane passing on the field.

She looked at her mother. "D . . . Dwaine?"

Clara nodded. "That was his last landing but I don't think you're in any condition . . ."

The statement was left uncompleted because her daughter had risen awkwardly and started out toward the parking area.

"Oh God." the mother moaned.

As she moved, self-consciously through the crowd and stepped over the rope barrier, Katie became aware of the renewed interest her presence created.

"Hey! It's the girl!" one youngster shouted.

"I told you she was gonna fly." another boasted.

Then the announcement came. "Our final contestant is Katie Stuart from Smithfield. Katie's been flying for about three months. She thinks all this airplane needs is a woman's touch."

He was teasing—drawing attention to her and she wished he wouldn't. Out of the corner of her eye she saw the people gathering behind the barrier. Children came running to squeeze in front. They watched the tall girl curiously.

"Go get 'em, Katie!" yelled a young woman from the crowd.

"You can do it!" a second joined in.

Katie recognized Shelly and a girl named Zelma— another one of "those girls" from North Cache High. They were dressed almost alike in flowery full skirts with off-the-shoulder, white blouses. Bright red lips and rouge cheeks stood out from, otherwise, pale complexions. Smiling and coquettish, they were hanging onto the arms of men who Katie knew were old—at least twenty-five.

So that's my cheering section, she thought, wryly. Fellow travelers. Well, what the hell! She waved to them.

From the cardboard box next to the building, she got three rolls of toilet paper and was waiting when Dwaine taxied up. He cut the engine and climbed out to a lusty round of applause. The bashful little boy grin, that Katie knew so well, appeared as he raised his hand to the crowd.

Damn, but he is good-looking! With her head lowered, Katie watched him and then glanced again at Shelly.

"Come on," he said, "I'll give you a hand."

After she was seated and her rolls of paper stowed, he lingered by the open door.

"Remember, after you drop the paper you have to turn more than half a circle to get back to it, but delay your turn for a few seconds." He showed her a grin. "Gives your more time to find the streamer after you roll out of your turn."

She studied his face—touched that he was offering advice and really wanted to help her.

"And you'll need to lose a little altitude at the same time or else you'll fly over it."

Still he remained. "As for the ribbon pickup, fly the prop directly at it, then pull up at the last second like Crow said, but not too hard. You don't want to stall."

He put a hand on her shoulder. "You're going to do swell, girl. Smooth, precision flying. Keep that in mind. Smooth precision flying like he told us."

Then, quite suddenly, he bent inside, kissed her on the forehead and winked. "Okay! Switch off, throttle closed."

She made the preparations mechanically, with her head spinning, as he walked to the front of the airplane. In position, he pulled the propeller through twice and gave the commands.

"Switch on, brakes, throttle cracked!"

At her nod, he flipped the blade downward. The engine fired on the first turn, barking through the short exhaust stacks. Dwaine waved and stepped aside.

Without conscious thought she applied throttle and began taxiing.

Maybe he really does like me, she thought. Maybe I'm not just another Shelly to him.

Putting into the runup area, she performed the preflight checks with quick, deft hands and comprehensive eyes. It occurred to her, at that moment, that she felt completely comfortable with the Cub—that all apprehension had disappeared. Everything about the airplane felt natural and familiar. Her confidence blossomed.

I wonder, she asked herself, if that means I really am a pilot—not just someone who can fly an airplane, but honestly and truly a pilot?

She smiled with the realization. I'm not a scared little girl anymore and I'm not just another of Dwaine's conquests—another Shelly. I'm more than that. I'm me! Katie "Stutterin' Stuart", but goddammit, I am a pilot!

Her checks completed, she steered the airplane expertly into alignment with the strip where she paused, momentarily, to regard the crowd of spectators—people whose total attention was now focused on her. "Take a g . . . good look," she told them. "Here we c . . . come—Mister P . . . Pi . . . Piper and me!"

Chapter 23

Second Lieutenant Sanford (Sandy) W. Strouthers, US. Army Air Corps, was developing a sizable headache—a throbbing that was almost synchronized with the pulse of the bomber's engines. The Lieutenant was also a little bit frightened by his present situation, although to suggest the possibility that he feared anything animal, mineral, vegetable or the supernatural, was to invite violent disagreement. On more than a few occasions, this point had been emphatically demonstrated. Sandy had a very short fuse and that was part of his undoing. He didn't have the size to backup his aggressive temperament. Consequently, his light-complexioned features were often marred with cuts, bruises, scrapes and bumps. What he lacked in bulk and pugilistic skills, however, was more than offset by sheer tenacity. He simply wore down his opponents—often they quit out of concern for doing him serious harm.

Testiness, by itself, can often be forgiven by superior officers, but not when coupled with a highly opinionated and cynical nature. He had no patience with the military way of life and few reservations about expressing himself on the subject. This had almost cost him his commission and killed any possibility for promotion to a higher rank until . . . (to quote his commanding officer), ". . . you're stumbling over a long, gray beard."

Aside from his pilot's wings, his outstanding ability as a navigation instructor excused him from being a permanent resident in the stockade.

In spite of his arrogance and self-assertiveness, he was well liked by his compatriots, who overlooked his quirks and laughed at his satirical denunciation of the Army, in general and the Air Corps in particular.

"You should have been born Irish," one friend told him. "Then you'd have a good excuse for being nuts."

On this late winter's evening, he was thoroughly pissed-off. More so than usual. Since being inducted, Sandy's disposition ranged from "bent-out-of-shape" to something beyond "thoroughly pissed-off". He was convinced that the Army kept the troops in a mean mood on purpose so they were ready to kill on command.

No damn chance for a sighting, he told himself ducking out of the bomber's Plexiglas bubble. Black as a witch in a coal bin. Tops must be at least twenty-thousand. Didn't know clouds went that high in this part of the country. Much more poking around in this crud we'll start picking up ice— if we're not already.

Making his way forward to the navigator's table, he stowed the sextant and then stared at the lines he had made on the chart. His youthful face was faintly illuminated by the red map light.

Jeesus! Ain't this the shits! he seethed inwardly. One damn mag don't check quite perfect so now here we are, almost six hours late. Should've scrubbed. If it'd been up to me, we would've scrubbed, orders or no orders.

The big airplane rocked in a sudden turbulence. This interrupted his thoughts until he had settled on the seat and fastened the safety belt.

I'd have told the Limies if they wanted this goddamn thing so bad, they could come and get it. A pilot with any balls would've let those assholes know where they could stick it.

He rubbed his hands together, vigorously, in a vain effort to restore some heat, then picked up the B-6. After checking the time, the altitude and the temperature, he rotated the scale on the instrument, studied the results and made a new mark on the chart.

"Ain't this the shits!" he repeated aloud, though it made little difference with a big Pratt and Whitney engine pounding away on each side of the fuselage. No idea what kind of winds we've got. Could've blown us into Arkansas since the last weather report. Now with the radio turned belly up, it's any body's guess where we are.

He stared gloomily at the chart trying to visualize how the elements would be affecting the airplane's passage through the night sky. What a hell of a time to have the radio crap out. Just my damn luck to get into a fix like this. Shouldn't have let 'em talk me into it.

With numbed fingers he fumbled with the headset connector. If it hadn't been for a chance to see Mildred in Chicago ... The thought of her warm softness almost diverted his attention from his misery. Boy, what a set of knockers.

He pressed the microphone button. "Can't see a thing to get a fix on, skipper." (He managed to make "skipper" sound like a dirty word.) "You may as well go back down and see if we can get under these clouds—maybe hold it at sixty-five degrees for a while."

He heard the reply in the headphones. "R ... r ... roger."

The copilot snorted. What kind of a Pilot-in-Command is that? he said to himself. Probably scared shitless. That's what they've got ferrying their goddamn airplanes and that's what I'm playing second fiddle to. A skirt. Can you believe it? A skirt! Those bastards are doing this to me just to kick my ass. Maybe she has more flying time than me, but she's still just a skirt. Serve 'em right if she scatters this son of a bitching thing all over the state of Kansas.

In the cockpit, Katie set the throttles and props for reduced power, adjusted the trim and returned her concentration to the faintly illuminated instruments.

Should be able to get under this stuff at three-thousand feet or so, she counseled herself. Not much danger of running into anything—it's all flat grain fields down there. Nothin' higher than a gopher's ears. If we can get out of this crap, we'll probably be able to spot Topeka or Kansas City. Go on into Sherman for some fuel, get the radio looked after, catch a few winks and still might get there in time. British don't take it over until tomorrow afternoon.

Her eyes scanned the instruments in sequence without thinking: artificial horizon, directional gyro, rate-of-climb, altimeter and airspeed. Occasionally she glanced at the engine instruments and the fuel indicators.

Wouldn't General "Hap" shit his britches if he knew one of Cochran's WASPS was flying blind . . . and at night, yet.

Army Air Corps General, Henry H. Arnold, had made it a condition that Jacqueline Cochran's women pilots fly only during daylight hours and visual contact conditions.

A smile crossed her face at the thought. What's the use of all that instrument training if we were never expected to use it? Hell! We logged more "blind" time than most of the combat pilots. Sure glad I've stayed current. The smile disappeared with this thought. I'd sure be up shit creek now, if I hadn't stayed current. Have to write Margie and tell her how the instrument training is paying off.

The memory of hours spent "flying the gauges" in the North American AT-6's with an instructor and then later with her pal, Margie, brought a lump to her throat. The fun we had, me and the rest of the "Woofteds", at Howard Hughes Field in Houston. In spite of all the hard work, the training, and the discipline in the "Women's Flying Training Detachment" (WFTD), there'd still been good times. There had been laughing and teasing and fun. Fun! Just like Amelia Earhart promised. Now the gals were stationed all over the country. Only me and Alice on this assignment."

She missed the others. They were the best girl friends she'd ever had—much more so than any of the kids back home. Those girls didn't share her interest in flying. All they wanted to talk about were boys and clothes. She'd found them boring and after she entered the Civilian Pilot Training program, she saw less and less of them. Most were married by that time, anyway, and the married ones were even more boring.

Now there was hardly anyone back in Cache Valley she cared about seeing except her mother and the Johnsons. Crow was running a flying school in California. Bing had been shot down in North Africa—she prayed that he was alive. Tweet was in England and, according to Dwain's last letter in her flight bag, he was still flying Hellcats in the Pacific. He'd written that he worried about her ferrying airplanes all over the country. Remembering gave her a warm feeling for his concern, although she couldn't help but grin at the irony of the situation.

My God! she thought. Him worried about me. No-body's shooting at me! Hell, I could be with Mary back at Camp Davis towing a target for gunnery practice. Her last letter said that the tow plane was hit more than the sleeve. Or I could be one of those Russian women, like Valentina what's-her-nameski, flying combat missions. Then he'd have something to worry about. All I do is drive an airplane from here to there.

Dwaine. She wondered if they would ever be more than the good friends, sometimes lovers, that they were now. Maybe if they could spend more time together it would be different, but there was a war on. At the same time, she couldn't imagine herself, back in Smithfield, as the wife of a feed store owner. Not after all she'd seen and done. There wasn't any other gal, that she knew of, from Smithfield, Utah who had been all over the United States—many of the big cities—had dinner with high-ranking generals, been introduced to lots of important people. Even a senator. And she had talked to a real live movie actor, Jimmy Stewart, now a major in the Army Air Corps. He'd, jokingly, suggested that they might be related until they'd compared the spelling of their names.

"Way back in time, there in the British Isles, we might've had the same ancestors before they started foolin' around with the spellin'." He'd given her one of his lopsided smiles.

"Then m . . . maybe I should be call . . . calling you 'Uncle Jimmy'," she'd told him with a mischievous grin.

"Hey! I'm not that old! Make it 'cousin'!"

They had laughed together. Then he'd kissed her on the forehead and said, with his characteristic drawl, "I'm sure I couldn't be more proud of you if you were my niece or cousin. You young women are doin' one hell of a fine job."

The remainder of that day, Katie had flown without being airborne.

After experiences like those, she decided, Smithfield would be pretty dull—even with Dwaine there. He was sweet, though, and he did help to bring me out of my shell, she thought, but then a lot of things changed after the contest.

* * *

The Contest—the tingling sensation and the excitement she'd felt that day, were still with her five years later. They'd carried her on their shoulders, Dwaine and the others, carried her while she chattered like a magpie—asking if it was true she'd won and demanding to know they weren't teasing her. And she'd hardly stopped talking since. The stutter was mostly gone, except when she was nervous.

Like right now, she thought.

The Contest: She had been over the details in her mind so many times that she could bring into focus every image, every spoken word, every feeling that she had experienced that day. Those were indelibly etched into her memory.

I'll never forget it, she thought. That may have been the best flying I've ever done. She remembered feeling that her body was part of the aircraft. She'd felt the air flowing over the long wings, sensed the pull of the propeller, knew intimately the coordination between rudder, aileron and elevator that produced perfect control.

Smooth, precision flying, she'd reminded herself and when she'd rolled level after the turn, the paper streamer was directly in front of the propeller. Smooth precision flying, she'd repeated later and found the ribbon fluttering behind the wheels. Smooth precision flying, she'd told herself later while flying an exact pattern for landing.

She remembered thinking that she'd done well, but had been too busy to calculate her score. On her last landing, she'd been too high and had to slip the airplane to lose altitude. Then, deciding she was too low, she'd been about to add power when she'd spotted Dwaine, standing alongside the strip, signaling with his arms, as Crow had done, to hold the plane off. She thought she'd landed short, but they told her later the tail wheel had hit the wide line and thrown up a cloud of calcimine—a perfect one-hundred points.

And then the boys had carried her, through all the people applauding, reaching up to shake her hand and calling congratulations. She wondered, later, if she stuttered while she was bantering with her fellow pilots and thanking those around her for their compliments. Probably did, she decided later, but it didn't matter at the time. When they'd put her on the ground, she'd seen the tears streaming down her mother's face and heard Crow's voice break into an amplified croak in the midst of a narration concerning his only girl student pilot. And then a wave of emotion had washed over her bringing on her own tears. As they'd clasped hands, she remembered saying to her mother, "what are you b . . . bawling about? I w . . . won! I won!" and they had stood, laughing at each other, crying with each other.

Yes indeed, she recalled. Everything certainly had changed after the Contest.

The Herald Journal had shown her picture along with a short article which described her as "another Earhart", comparing her tall, slender form and close-cropped, blond hair with that of the famous aviatrix.

Her senior year at North Cache High had been, at least, tolerable. A new self-assurance had given her the courage to continue talking and accept the teasing with grace. That had gained her a few friends and the attention she received from the contest earned her the respect of others.

She'd continued flying, of course, although not as frequently nor as intently. Her mother had provided a small allowance, in addition to the money that Bart paid for her part-time help with chores. This had been adequate to pay for some solo flight time almost every Sunday—particularly since Crow had remained generous extending credit when needed.

During "beet-vacation" she'd had an opportunity to supplement her dwindling funds by topping sugar beets. Most of the young men at North Cache and other high schools, had been committed to this yearly chore during the two-week scheduled recess. Anything that they could do, she could do also, Katie had figured.

Bart had, at first, objected. "That's damn heavy work for a girl." He'd finally relented as a result of her persistent wheedling.

To her dismay, Katie had learned that the farmer was telling the truth. Beet-thinning had been tiring but not, necessarily, strenuous work. Topping was savage. Instead of a stub-handled hoe, a very large knife, with a hook at the end of the blade, was used. The worker straddled the row of beets, which had been lifted out of the ground by a potato digger. This machine, drawn by horses or tractor, also shook loose the dirt and deposited the beets on the surface. The beet-topper's task involved using the hook on the knife to pick up a beet—some weighing six to eight pounds or more—and the sharp blade to chop away the leafy stock. Then the beets would be tossed in piles ready to be loaded into trucks or wagons for delivery to the beet dump at the railroad yard.

Katie had thought she would die from the work. At first she'd tried to keep pace with the men, but her arms had lacked the physical strength. This had been a blow to her pride. She soon learned, however, that by working steady she could almost keep up. Not allowing herself to stop, as the men did frequently, to talk and joke, enabled her to stay with the best of them by the end of the second week.

"My God, but she's a horse for work!" Bart had told his wife.

He'd paid her an unheard of dollar and a half a day.

The following summer had found her back in Bart's fields earning enough money to continue her training for a Private Pilot's license. She had her first taste of air travel, and the experience of landing at another airport, when Crow had flown with her to Pocatello, Idaho—a distance of eighty-nine miles—for her dual cross-country instruction. Planning the flight, plotting the course, memorizing the route and checkpoints, calculating the heading and flight time had been so stimulating she'd hardly slept the night before.

Afterwards, she had spent very little time flying in the valley and had chosen, instead, to explore in every direction except east. The Wasatch Range still represented an imposing barrier to the little airplane.

Following the Bear River out of the valley to where it flowed into the Great Salt Lake, she'd continued on to Ogden and, another time, to Salt Lake City. Then one warm day in early August, with her confidence soaring, she had taken a western heading and intercepted the highway that led to Burley, Idaho. The long trek over the bleak terrain had been one she didn't want to repeat. Turbulence, produced by thermals rising from the hot desert floor, had caused the Cub to rock and pitch violently so that Katie's energy had been drained in attempting to hold the craft level.

After landing, she'd wisely accepted the local operator's advice to wait until evening for the return flight.

Finally, the lure to the east had overcome her caution and one beautiful quiet morning, without telling her instructor, she'd ventured over the mountains to see the Bear Lake and her home town of Garden City from the air.

The little Cub had seemed eager as its pilot, climbing to eight-thousand feet over Logan canyon. After passing Naomi Peak, looming another two-thousand feet above her altitude, Katie had seen the formidable ridge she must cross to reach her destination and began to doubt the wisdom of her undertaking. Her fears had been groundless, however. Mister Piper proved equal to the task. The sight of the beautiful Bear Lake coming into view, as she swept over this final obstruction, had caused her breath to catch in her throat.

Then there'd been the exhilarating ride down the eastern slope of the Wasatch Range toward the blue waters.

For a while she'd soared a few-hundred feet above the beach, searching for her past and wondering at the sense of loss she felt. Later she'd tried to catch sight of the little farm but hadn't been able to find it. Too much time had passed.

These excursions had extracted a terrible toll on her earnings, even though Bart had increased her pay by fifty percent over the previous year. But then her expenditures had also taken a jump, especially since she'd begun giving more attention to her appearance for Dwaine's benefit. Clothes and cosmetics took on a greater importance during her senior year at North Cache High. Katie suffered through many agonizing decisions in trying to establish her economic priorities. Then she'd found a solution to her dilemma.

Since Dwaine had already acquired his Private Pilot's license, Katie coaxed him into taking her on cross-country flights. The Pontiac coupe had stopped by for her, at the little house on the edge of town, almost every Sunday morning. On those occasions, she'd brought along a picnic sack and he, a blanket. A blanket, she remembered. Just like a man! Her mother thought he was gorgeous.

She'd enjoyed the ride in the front seat, with the greatly improved view it afforded. Using chart and plotter, she guided the flight of the craft along each path that whim and circumstance determined.

Katie smiled with the inner glow she felt recalling those wonderful memories—of flying off in new directions with new scenes and new adventures waiting. They'd searched out and found secluded meadows where they spread the blanket on the grass under the Cub's wing. Here they had lain, engaging in the tender teasing and touching of youth. Seems like I was always afraid of getting knocked-up, she remembered.

And they'd walked and explored and held hands— talking endlessly of everything and nothing.

But the summer ended and, in the fall, she'd entered the Agricultural College at Logan for only one purpose—to be eligible to participate in Roosevelt's Civilian Pilot Training program. Clara had been pleased that her daughter was seeking higher education and Katie saw no reason to set her straight.

Crow had shown her an article in the Herald Journal that told of a proposal by Bob Hinkley for using colleges and universities to administer the C.P.T. program. Hinkley, a fixed-base operator from Ogden, who'd been appointed to the Civilian Aviation Authority, was suggesting that these institutions provide ground school instruction and contract the flying instruction with local aviation firms. It had been a long wait for the college to be accepted into the program but when it happened, Katie was one of the first—and the only girl—to sign up. She'd had to ask Bart for a forty-dollar advance on future earnings to cover the lab fee but then, at government expense, she finally completed her requirements for a Private Pilot's license.

True to her word, she had taken Bart as her first passenger—an excursion over the Cache National forest looking for elk. Crow, in the meantime, kept Duke's attention diverted catching the ball. No matter how old, the big dog never seemed to tire of the game.

Later, she'd qualified for the advanced training course and went on to become a flight instructor. That didn't last long. The War Department decided that CPT members had to be part of the military so Katie's short career was ended.

After the war started, with Bing, Tweet and Bob enlisted in the Army Air Corps and Dwaine flying for the Navy, Katie had cursed being a woman and, therefore, denied the privilege of serving her country by flying. Then she'd heard about woman pilots being recruited to ferry airplanes in the British Isles—known as the "Air Transport Auxiliary". She'd made inquiries, but had been informed she didn't have enough flying experience. At that time she'd accumulated only two-hundred, eighty-seven hours and fifteen minutes. She'd been rejected by the "Woman's Ferrying Squadron" (WAFS) for the same reason. Her shattered pride had finally been salvaged by her acceptance into the "Women's Flying Training Detachment" (WFTD), organized by the famous aircraft racing pilot, Jacquelin Cochran. Later the organization was renamed "Women's Airforce Service Pilots" (WASPs).

Four-thousand feet, Katie noted. Should be breaking out soon. Her eyes flicked from the instrument panel to the windshield and back. Not yet. Don't want to get much below three-thousand.

She made some adjustments to the throttles and lowered the flaps to slow the rate of descent. After trimming the aircraft, she switched on the landing lights and anxiously glanced at the windshield again.

Katie Stuart, you dumb shithead! she scolded herself, what are you doing here?

Her answer was a wry grin. You know damn well what you're doing here, she thought. In spite of the tiredness, the boredom of waiting around, sleeping on air terminal or depot benches, wearing the same clothes for days on end and in spite of the times when it's scary—like right now—you wouldn't be doing anything else. They just pat you on the back, tell you what a swell job you're doing, what a fine pilot you are and you're all set to do it again. Girl, they've sure got your number!

A faint line of light in the windshield caught her eyes at that moment. She pushed the microphone button. "Lieutenant! We're under the clouds. Looks like a city up ahead."

He came forward quickly and peered through the windshield. "Might be Kansas City."

She nodded and raised the flaps. "We'll put into the first decent-sized airport we come to. I need to go to the can something fierce."

He gave her a big grin. She's okay! he decided slipping into the copilot's seat.

Katie returned the grin. Kinda cute, she thought. "Want to fly it?" She gestured toward the control column in front of him.

"Naw. You're doing alright," he said. "Actually you fly a pretty good compass course . . . ," then added, ". . . for a girl."

Her eyebrows lifted. "For a girl, huh?"

He was watching the approaching lights, his expression bland. "For a girl," he repeated. "Hey! Whatcha doin'?"

She had begun slowly rotating the control yoke, left and right, so the long wings of the bomber were alternately rising and dipping.

"I'm going to make you sick," she said smiling wickedly.

"That'll be the day." he replied.

But the thoughts of Katie Stuart, Pilot-in-Command, had turned to another time, another place and another airplane whose yellow wings had cast a magic spell on a girl in a pasture.